I didn't know exactly what to expect from her. She'd been married, divorced. All that made her seem older, even though she really wasn't much older than me. She didn't seem the type you'd make out with in a car. I turned the motor off and we just sat there. It was a hot night. I hoped I hadn't gotten too sweaty bowling.

I hesitated. "You know, you shouldn't smoke so much."

"Yeah, I know. I have a lot of bad habits." Then she turned and smiled at me. "Do you?"

"What?" I wanted to kiss her, but wasn't sure how to begin.

"Tell me about your bad habits," Audrey said, moving closer.

"I don't have any," I admitted. "I stay in good shape, I run, I eat properly. . . ."

"How about girls?"

"I like girls." That sounded dumb, but I went on, "I—I like you."

"So kiss me, okay?"

———————

FAWCETT JUNIPER BOOKS
By Norma Klein:

ANGEL FACE

BEGINNERS' LOVE

IT'S OKAY IF YOU DON'T LOVE ME

LOVE IS ONE OF THE CHOICES

THE QUEEN OF THE WHAT IFS

# GIVE AND TAKE

## Norma Klein

FAWCETT JUNIPER • NEW YORK

For Daniel Zitin

# 1

Rob said he'd promised Linc we'd come by Sunday afternoon to see him, Taffy, and the baby. "What for?" I asked.

I thought of Linc and Taffy and how miserable they looked at the party after our high school graduation last month. They'd gotten his mother to babysit for the baby, but you could tell they weren't having a good time. Linc got drunk and Taffy kept showing baby pictures to everyone. It really cast a pall over the evening. Rob, Linc, and I have been buddies since fifth grade. You can't help feeling for a guy when he gets roped into a situation like that. There but for the grace of God, maybe.

"Well, you know how it is," Rob said. "He's feeling kind of cut off. Like, here we are, out in the world, free, all that . . . and he's got this wife, this kid . . ."

"Whose fault is that?" I asked. I didn't mind seeing Linc so much, but just sitting around with Taffy and the baby didn't seem like the most exciting way to spend the afternoon.

"Nobody's fault," Rob said. "It just happened. God's will or something."

"She wanted to get knocked up so he'd marry her, that's all," I said. "That wasn't God's will, it was Taffy's will."

"That contraceptive stuff doesn't always work," Rob said. "Nothing's foolproof."

"Maybe. But I know one thing. When I do it with someone, she better have something she can show me that I *know* works."

"What've you got against Taffy?" Rob said. "You went together once, didn't you?"

"Yeah, but that was junior high. We were just kids. . . . He's just gone and wrecked his life, if you ask me."

Rob crossed his arms. "So, what would *you* have done? Just gone off and left her?"

"Listen," I told him. "There are millions of couples who want babies. They could've given it up for adoption."

"Yeah, that's true," Rob said. "But you know, we're judging it from our point of view. Maybe they're happy."

"You just said how he was feeling cut off and all," I pointed out.

"That's the point. To him our lives seem so great. But what's so great about them? Do we have such fantastic sex lives?"

"It'll be different in college." I feel certain of that. Rob is going to Wayne State, where his father went; I'm going to the University of Michigan.

"It's the same thing," Rob said gloomily. "First

you find a girl, you go through a whole thing. If she gets serious, you either marry her or you dump her and feel like a schmuck."

"You're thinking of high school," I said. "College girls are different. There're more different types. A lot of them are just looking to have some fun because they want to get started in careers, just like us."

"I'll believe it when I see it."

Linc was out in the yard with the baby when we came over. They're living with his parents so his mother can look after the kid some of the time. The baby was in a hammock, awake, but not screaming. All the other times I saw it, it was screaming.

"What's wrong? Is it sick?" I asked.

"His name is Webster," Linc said, annoyed, "not It. . . . No, he's not sick. He's fine."

"How come he's so quiet, then?" I asked. The baby looked at me with big, round, dark eyes.

Linc laughed. "They don't cry *all* the time. It just seems like it." Linc is a short guy, five four or five, but really built. Maybe because he's so short, he figured he had to do something to make up for it, so he lifted weights all through school. He has a very broad chest and short hairy legs.

Rob was standing, staring at the baby. "I thought it was a girl," he said.

"What's with you guys?" Linc said. "Don't you pay attention to anything?"

"I thought if it was a boy, it had to wear blue," Rob said. "That's what my mother said."

"I happen to come from a family with all male descendents," Linc said proudly. "So he couldn't have been a girl. No way."

"How about your mother?" I asked.

"That doesn't count," he said. "Anyhow, even in her family it's the same, except for her. She was the exception."

"To what?" Taffy asked, coming down on the porch steps. She was carrying a tray with a pitcher of lemonade and some glasses. Taffy's cute, a little thin, never wears a bra. Up until tenth grade she always wore glasses and had her hair in a pony tail. Then she got contacts and started wearing her hair loose down her back, but whenever I see her, I remember her the way she was before.

"These jerks thought Web was a girl," Linc said, pointing to us.

Taffy looked wistful. "I know, I kept hoping for a girl, some little cute, fluffy girl."

"Only we got lucky," Linc said.

Taffy turned red. "How is that lucky? Girls are lucky." She turned to me. "Wouldn't you have wanted a girl, Spence?"

I shrugged. "Sure, that would've been okay." Maybe cause Taffy and I went out for about six months in junior high, sometimes she still acts flirtatious when I'm around. Or maybe it's just to get Linc's goat, to show him other guys find her attractive.

"He has four sisters," Linc said. "What does *he* know?"

"My mother wanted a boy," I said, taking a glass of lemonade Taffy handed me.

"Well, sure," Taffy said. "She had four girls already! That's completely different. If I had four girls, I'd want a boy, too."

"Hey Taff, you didn't put any sugar in this," Linc said, wrinkling his nose.

"I did so!"

4

"Well, not enough. It's all sour. Go get some more."

She stuck her chin in the air. "*You* go get some more. You have legs."

Linc glared at her. "These are my guests, okay? They came over to see me."

Taffy looked at us. "I thought they came over to see *us*." After a second she said, "Oh, I'll get the fucking sugar."

The porch door slammed. Rob and I just kind of looked at the ground.

"Girlfriends and wives are a whole different thing," Linc said. "Let me tell you."

"Yeah, well . . ." I didn't exactly know what to say. I don't have either one, so I can't say.

"Girlfriends do what you say, they look up to you. Then overnight they change." He stared at us gloomily. "Appreciate your freedom. I wish I had when I'd had it."

"Nobody appreciates anything when they have it," Rob said. "It's like probably you don't appreciate being alive till you're dead."

We both looked at him. Rob comes out with these really peculiar comments some times.

"How's Emmy Lou?" Linc asked me.

"Don't know. We broke up."

Linc was staring at me with that same gloomy expression. We used to call him Spider because of that and his long hairy arms. "Did you do it with her or what?"

I turned red because right then Taffy was coming down the steps, and she has ears like an elephant. "Uh-uh," I muttered.

"She wanted to," Taffy said, dumping a whole lot

of sugar in the pitcher right from a two-pound box. "She told us all she would've."

"Girls say a lot of stuff," Linc said. "Half of it they don't even mean."

"Why shouldn't she want to do it with him?" Taffy said. She smiled at me. "I bet lots of girls would've, even ones he never knew about."

Luckily Linc didn't seem to notice that remark, but I was really beginning to feel uncomfortable. Rob broke in with, "In college it'll be different. Girls with careers and everything." He's like that. I tell him something, just to express an opinion, and two minutes later he's accepted it as fact.

"Is that what *you* want, Spence?" Taffy asked earnestly. "A girl with a career?"

"I don't really know exactly," I said, wishing she wouldn't stare at me so hard.

"And you'll do half everything?" she went on. "Half of the cooking? Half of the grocery shopping?"

"That would be—" I started. But before I could finish she broke in, turning to Linc, "See, Spence wants a modern marriage! He wants to do half of everything."

"He didn't even finish his sentence," Linc said disgustedly.

Just then the baby started to cry. Taffy scooped him up with one arm and hugged him. "That's okay," she said. "You're just hungry, aren't you, little sweetie? Are you hungry?" She started unbuttoning her shirt.

Linc reached out and touched her arm. "Do that inside, will you, Taff?"

"No!" She pulled back. "Why should I do it inside? It's a perfectly natural process. What's there to be ashamed of? They've never seen tits before?"

Rob and I looked at each other. "Actually, maybe we ought to go," Rob said.

"See!" Linc said. "They just got here, they didn't even finish their lemonade, and now they're going because they're embarrassed that—"

"They're embarrassed that you're acting like an asshole," Taffy said. The baby had already latched onto her nipple and was drinking from it. "Are *you* embarrassed, Spence? 'Cause if you are, I'll go inside."

"No, it's okay, it doesn't bother me. I've seen my sisters do it lots of times."

Taffy sat down and shifted the baby into a more comfortable position. It's true, it's different if it's a girl you've known from school than if it's your sister. I have to admit, I still find Taffy appealing—I guess it's that there's something gentle and delicate about her that makes you want to take care of her, protect her. But she's Linc's wife now—out of bounds. I tried to not look at her while she was nursing.

"You're the one who said I *should* nurse in the first place," she said to Linc, "and now you make such a big fuss about it."

Linc got up and stomped into the house. Taffy looked after him. "Boy, is he stubborn!" she said. "You do one minor, irrelevant thing that he doesn't like, and he sulks for a whole day, a whole week even sometimes!" She looked down at the baby who seemed to have fallen asleep. "So, what're you guys doing for the summer? Did you get jobs?"

Rob told her about his job at Woolworth's, in the tool department. I told her how I sometimes help out my brother-in-law, Mercer, who's a contractor. "I'm

7

not in the union so they don't pay me regular wages, but it's something."

"Want to hold him?" Taffy asked, me, once she'd buttoned up her blouse. "He won't wake up. He sleeps real soundly."

Since she was holding the baby out to me, I took him. "I bet you've had a lot of experience with babies, with your sisters and all," she said. "You're holding him just right."

I still felt funny, with Linc having stormed off. "He's cute," I said lamely.

"Yeah, he's good. He's a good baby," Taffy said, with a sad expression. "Only I just don't know." Then she brightened up. "Hey, listen, I meant to say, if you ever want to double-date or triple-date or whatever, we'd be glad to. Linc's mom can sit. Just 'cause we're married doesn't mean we never go out or anything."

"I'm not dating anyone special at the moment," I said.

"Oh, it doesn't have to be anyone special," Taffy said. "Just anyone."

I cleared my throat. "No, I mean, I'm not dating anyone period."

"Oh . . . well, if you are or, you know, just call us up, okay?"

"Sure," I said.

Rob was just standing there, in one of his trances. "I guess we better be going," he said. "Thanks for the lemonade, Taffy."

"Was it too sweet?" she asked, putting the baby back in the hammock. "Linc likes it so sweet! It's terrible for his teeth. I tell him that. He's got nine hundred cavities already."

Actually, it had been horribly sweet after she

8

dumped in all the extra sugar. "Sugar's not that good for you," I said, "in large amounts."

"You're smart," Taffy said admiringly. "You know what's good for you. You eat right, you stay thin. . . . He doesn't listen, that's all." She leaned over and gave us each a quick hug. "Thanks for coming."

Rob and I walked down the street to where we had to get the bus. It was hot, but the sun had gone in and the air felt heavy, like it might rain. "Maybe we should've gone in and said goodbye to Linc," Rob said. "I mean, we came over to see him."

"He didn't seem in such a good mood."

Rob looked thoughtful. He has a lot of freckles, and in the summer they almost blur into each other. "I think Taffy's a nice person," he said. "And a good mother. Only I know how he felt. I don't know if I'd want my wife nursing in front of other guys. Would you?"

"It wouldn't bother me," I said.

"It just makes you start thinking of other things," Rob said.

Actually, the only thing that bothered me was the way Taffy seemed to be flirting with me. But maybe it was just my imagination. I kept thinking of all those funny little notes she used to send me in fourth grade. One of them Billy Rodgers found in her desk. She'd written it with her friend, Lucie. It said:

*Dares*

1. Kiss Spencer in class
2. Start rumor that you went out with Spencer
3. Pull him in the closet
4. Call him up on the phone and tell him you love him

5. Write him a love letter
6. Invite him to your house

Not that they ever did any of those things. I guess they just had vivid imaginations.

I never took advantage of Taffy's liking me. What I mean is, I probably wouldn't have started asking her out if she hadn't made all the first moves, but I really liked her. It's just it always made me uncomfortable that she liked me so much more than I liked her. She'd look at me with this totally adoring, almost worshipful expression, and it made me feel as much guilty as flattered. I was basically relieved when Linc started dating her. He asked me if I'd mind and I told him truthfully no.

"If I have a wife, ever," Rob said suddenly. "I don't even want her to nurse. It makes their tits hang way down after a while."

"Who says?" Rob has a million theories like that he always claims to have read somewhere.

"It's a medically proven fact." That's his usual answer. "Well, would you?"

"Would I what?"

"Let whoever you were married to nurse like that?"

"Sure, it's cheaper than bottles."

Rob looked grim. "You don't even care how she looks? I want someone with a good figure that stays good permanently, and that's final."

"You shouldn't have broken up with Edina, then." She had a great figure, though that was about all, in my opinion.

"Right, maybe I shouldn't have. . . . But you said we'd do so much better in college, better-quality girls."

I sighed. "How about the summer?"

"I'm double-dating with my dad tonight. Maybe something'll come of that. The only thing is, he always gets first pick and he always picks the best one."

"Aren't they too old for you?" I asked. "In their twenties or whatever?"

"They don't know my real age. Dad adds a couple of years to my age and takes a couple of years off his. That way it sort of evens out."

I don't have a father. My parents died in a car crash when I was just two, so I don't even remember them. I have four sisters and they all live in our town, but they're a lot older than me. The youngest one, Lizzie, is twenty-four. She lives with Dan, the basketball coach at our high school. Lizzie's the sexiest of my sisters, the most fun-loving and impulsive. She's gotten engaged to a bunch of weird guys, but my other sisters always talk her out of marrying them. June is real quiet and shy. She used to be a nun, but she left the convent about five years ago.

Carnie's the most athletic. She and Mercer, my brother-in-law, don't have kids yet, so she teaches during the school year and turns into a tennis bum in the summer. I can beat her, but she has a fantastic game for a woman. She serves just like a man! If I wanted to talk to someone about my problems, I'd pick Carnie. Willa's tall and bossy and religious. She's got two kids, but she's the one I like the best.

I see my sisters a lot, but I live with my grandparents, who raised me. Whenever people start talking about their fathers, complaining or anything, I think of my grandfather, who's seventy-eight and so grouchy he hardly ever talks except to complain about something. At meals he just sits there, staring out the window at the bird feeder, not seeming to hear what anyone says. If my grandmother leans forward and asks him if the food was all right, she usually has to ask around four times, and finally he'll say, "Edible." That's it. I never heard him say anything more than "edible." Sometimes she'll get all worried, afraid he's not eating enough, and she'll rush into the kitchen and make him something different from what everyone else is having. She always gives him the tenderest piece of meat, sometimes even cuts it up for him. My grandmother's a really kind, lovable person, and she's not stupid, so I guess at some point my grandfather must've been different than he is now or she wouldn't have fallen in love with him and lived with him for so many years. But sometimes I wonder.

Rob and I jumped on the bus and sat down toward the back. Neither of us said much on the way back to his house.

My sister June has saved up some money from her job. She's a private nurse who works in people's homes. What she wants to do with it is send my grandparents on a trip for their fiftieth wedding anniversary. Willa had invited us over one night when June sprang her idea.

"Where do you want them to go?" Willa asked. She's tall and overweight, with a big mound of hair stacked on top of her head. Her husband, Jake, a night cop, was on duty.

"Anywhere they want," June said. "They've never been anywhere." June speaks in such a low voice, it's hard to hear her sometimes. From the age of seventeen to twenty-three she was a nun. My grandmother is Catholic, though not that religious, but at the end of high school, June just suddenly announced that she wanted to enter a convent. My grandfather who, like I said, hardly ever says anything, got hysterical and said she was wrecking her life. She did it anyway and

13

after five years said it'd all been a mistake. Then she married a guy she'd only been dating three months, which, my grandfather said, showed sense—that she was finally realizing what her priorities ought to be. Only as it turned out her husband, Silas, ended up leaving her for another woman. Silas and his girlfriend live not far from my grandparents' house; I sometimes see them together. My grandfather says if *he* ever sees them, he's going to shoot them, but June says everyone has a right to their personal choice, and she hopes he's happy now, happier than he was with her.

"Maybe they'd want to go to some island," I suggested. "Grandma likes the beach."

June smiled at me. "That's what I thought, Spence. Some wonderful, warm, tropical place with white sand where you can lie and stare out at the ocean . . ." Her voice trailed off, like she was imagining it.

"You go," Willa said. "That's a better idea. You go, Junie."

June shrank back. "I don't want to go. It's for them."

"They're old. They can't appreciate it. You go, and maybe you'll meet someone."

June looked down at her plate. "I don't *want* to meet anyone. I've been married once. That's enough."

Willa has a big hearty voice, almost like a man. "You got a bad egg. Don't judge by him. There're lots of great guys out there."

"He wasn't a bad egg," June whispered, the way she does when she's upset.

"He was! Look, I'm not *blaming* him. Something went wrong. But the Bible says—"

14

June clamped her hands over her ears. "I don't want to hear about the Bible. Silas is a good, sweet person. He's *not* screwed up! And I want Grandma and Grandpa to have some fun while they still can."

Willa looked at me. "Don't *you* think he was screwed up, Spence? Be honest."

"I just think—" I started, when Roxanne, Willa's daughter, and her brother, Bo, came charging into the room.

"We'll talk about it later," Willa said.

"I liked Silas," Roxanne said. "You're just prejudiced, Mom."

"Yeah, right," Bo chimed in.

"You children leave us alone. We're talking about a family matter," Willa said stiffly.

"Send Great-Grandma to Africa," Bo said. "She can ride in a special car and see wild animals."

"Send her to Paris," Roxanne said. "She can buy perfume and go to the top of the Eiffel Tower."

"I said I want you two out of this room!" Willa bellowed. They each scooped up some candy from a bowl on the table and ran out.

June looked at me sideways. She has sad bluish-gray eyes. "Will you go buy the tickets, Spence? I'll give you the money."

"To where, though?"

"Ask the travel agent. Say you want a nice vacation for them, just two weeks or so. Grandpa gets tired so fast lately."

Willa gave a sigh. "We're in the middle of a terrible recession and you're just throwing good money down the drain. Grandpa'll want to come home on the second day. You know what he's like."

"It's for Gran," June said.

"Send her alone, then."

"She'd never *go* alone."

"True." Willa looked grave. "I wish Gran would have more fun out of life. She's only in her early seventies. She *looks* young."

"She's okay," June said. "So, will you do it, Spence? Just inquire at the agency. Let us know what the possibilities are."

I wish someone would send me off on a vacation like that, as a surprise. I think Willa's right. They'll probably go, stay about two or three days, my grandfather will complain about everything from the second he gets there—the food, the hotel. Or else he'll get sick. That happened once when I was little. We set off on some long trip and the same night we got there, he said his back was hurting him and we had to turn around and drive back.

After dinner Roxanne dragged me into her room to listen to a new song on an album she'd gotten by X: "I Should Not Think Bad Thoughts." Sometimes I give her my old albums, though our tastes are pretty different. "I think they have such good harmonies," she said. "I just love them."

I sat on the floor, looking at the album cover. "Yeah, nice."

What I kept thinking about was how when I was thirteen or fourteen, it seemed like I got bad thoughts all the time, no matter what I was doing. I couldn't control it. In class, when I was doing my homework, all the time. Not just about sex, but even worse things, wanting to kill people or just do stupid, destructive things. I got really scared I might do some of those things, but then I started practicing this mind control system from a book Rob lent me. It said when a bad thought comes to you, you should think of your mind like a metal shield and let the bad thought bounce off, not sink in. It said bad thoughts were in the atmosphere, waiting for a place to settle, and if they sense you're receptive, they'll come to you.

"How come you look so worried?" Roxanne said softly, when the song was over.

I shrugged. "College," I said, just to say something.

"Aren't you going?"

"Yeah, I'm going." I looked up at Roxanne. I worry about her sometimes because she's so funny-looking. She has bad skin and she dresses in a peculiar way, bright colors that don't match at all.

She sat down opposite me, looking right at me. "I wish someone liked me, some boy. Do you think they eventually will, Spence?"

"Sure," I said unsteadily. It was hot in her room; the windows were closed, and there was a funny smell.

"Mom thinks I'm backward because I haven't dated anyone yet, because I never go to parties. I just want one person, and if I loved them, I'd do whatever they wanted!" She stared at me with a scared, defiant expression.

"No, listen, Rox, don't do that," I said nervously. "Guys take advantage of girls who—"

"I *want* that to happen," she insisted. "I want to be totally in love so I merge with the other person. Did you ever do that?"

"What?" Sometimes she talks in such a strange way, I can't even follow her.

"Did you ever, like, totally merge with someone, so you felt like you were one person?"

"I wasn't sure if she meant sex or what. "I never—no."

"Don't you ever want to?"

I couldn't think of what to say. The record was over. It was going around and around. Roxanne jumped up to take it off. "Bad thoughts," she said, in a kind of a singsong. "*I should not have bad thoughts*." She laughed. "I love bad thoughts! They're exciting. Do you ever have them?"

"No." I lied, wanting to get out of the room fast.

She kept looking at me with an intent expression. "I have them about you sometimes," she said. "We've done just about everything you could possibly imagine together."

I jumped up. I felt uncomfortable. "Listen, Roxanne, don't—"

"They're just thoughts," she said. "Don't worry. I won't tell Mom or anyone. No one knows."

"I have this book on mind control," I said. "Maybe you—"

Roxanne laughed, clapping her hands together. "You wouldn't believe some of the things we did," she said.

I walked out of the room. Maybe she's crazy. God, I'm her uncle! She shouldn't even be having *thoughts* like that. I think I'll send her that book. When I got back, Willa and June were still arguing about the vacation. "I'll go on Monday," I promised them.

"Don't put money down," June said. "Just get some brochures."

Willa looked at me. "Has Roxanne been bothering you?" she said.

I turned red. "No, we were just listening to a new record she got."

18

"Those records are bad for kids," Willa said. "I'm telling you, they are not like what we used to listen to. They don't have melodies, they are scary songs. That girl has a twisted mind and she isn't fifteen yet."

"She's okay," I said.

The next day I had to go to RGC in the morning. That's the Michigan Repository for Germinal Choice. It's a sperm bank, and twice a week I go over there and donate some of my sperm to them. They pay you twenty-five dollars for each time, but I'm not doing it just for the money. I'm doing it to help all those women who normally couldn't have babies, like my sister Carnie, who's been trying to adopt for five years. Growing up with four sisters you hear a whole lot about female things—boyfriends, getting married, having kids. Sometimes I think I know more about women than a lot of guys who're twice my age. I know women worry about all this a lot. It can really make them unhappy.

Someday I'll probably have my own kids, but not for a long time, not till I'm thirty and established in my career. So until then I'm doing my part in keeping the world going. Even if, like Rob thinks, there'll be a nuclear holocaust and there won't be any more world,

I'll still have done my part. It's not so different from giving blood, in a way, only what you're giving here is more important: you're giving life.

What I do before I go is get up early, around six, and jog. Then I take a long shower, eat a light breakfast, and meditate. When I go into that little room I feel geared up, but in a good way. I think of that woman somewhere who's going to be so happy the day she finds out that my sperm has connected with her egg. She looks different on different days. Sometimes she has clothes on, sometimes not. She always has long, soft hair and beautiful breasts and a really kind, warm, friendly expression. Once she started crying, she was so happy. I guess what's strange is, I don't exactly imagine us doing it together. It's like I'm not even there, except that she feels my presence and she knows that we're uniting.

Afterward I walk down the street quietly and calmly, and I feel so good. The reason is I'm helping someone I don't even know. If I knew them, it would spoil it in a way.

Just before lunch I stopped in at the travel agency to inquire about two-week trips to the Caribbean. The girl behind the counter looked up at me. "When are you planning to go? It's very hot there now in July."

"It's not for me," I explained. "It's for my grandparents."

"Do they have a preference?" She had big hazel eyes that had a soft, blurry expression.

"They don't know about it yet. It's a surprise."

"Why don't you pull up a chair and I'll tell you about what we can offer you?"

I pulled up a chair. I saw she had a pin saying Ms. Rummel. Her hair was short and dark, with curly

22

bangs that fell forward around her ears. "What activities do your grandparents enjoy engaging in in their leisure time?" she asked.

"Not that much . . . my grandfather's almost eighty."

"Do they swim? Fish? Go dancing?"

"They'll probably just lie in the sun."

"St. Maarten's is beautiful," she said. "I went there with my boyfriend once. They have a beach where you can swim without your clothes. And, plus, they have a regular beach."

I started imagining her on that beach. "My grandparents would like just a regular place," I said, my heart pounding.

"Are you going with them?" she asked.

I shook my head.

"You'd love it there," she said. "You should go, too."

"I can't exactly afford it," I stammered. "I'm just . . . it's my sister's money."

She leaned forward and looked up at me, twisting her hair around her finger. "No one wears clothes so you don't feel uncomfortable. I'm usually really shy about showing my body to strangers, but there I wasn't. It just seemed like a natural thing to do."

"It sounds . . . healthy," I said.

"You get sunburned in funny places," she said. "That's the main problem. But only if you go out between noon and three."

She showed me some more pamphlets and said I could take them. "You know, I think I've seen you before. You work at the hospital, right?"

I hesitated. "Yeah, well I do tests for new drugs."

"I saw you waiting there a few times. I recognized

you because of that scar." She put her hand up and touched her eyebrow. I have a scar on my left eyebrow from an accident I was in when I was ten. Somehow, though she was just touching *her* eyebrow, I felt funny, as though she'd touched me.

"I fell off my bike when I was a kid," I said.

She smiled at me. "You're still a kid, aren't you?"

"I'm eighteen." If anything, people usually tell me I look old for my age.

"Hey, relax, I didn't mean—I guess I usually go for older men. You just look—you know, young. I'm eighteen, too. *I'm* a kid."

Somehow *she* looked older, maybe because she was sitting at a desk and had a real job. "When it happened, with the bike, I was just ten," I explained.

She stuck her pencil behind her ear. "What kind of drugs do you test?"

"Huh?" She spoke so fast I had a hard time following her.

"You said you test drugs over there. Isn't that dangerous?"

"Uh-uh." I bent the edge of the pamphlet back and forth. *I must not think bad thoughts.*

Ms. Rummel kept looking at me and twisting her hair around her finger. "I go over there on account of my cousin," she said. "She's an unwed mother. Or at least she wants to be. . . . Only this clinic they have—did you hear of it? They get women pregnant, only it's so prejudiced! Once they learned she wasn't married, they said no dice. Isn't that terrible? I said she should have just lied, but she didn't want to. That's what I'd do, not that I'm ever having kids."

I never heard of that before, only of the opposite, women who aren't married who try to get rid of them.

24

"What does she want a child for, if she isn't married?"

She shrugged. "Some biological thing. I don't know. Why does anyone want kids? They just scream a lot and wreck your life. I wouldn't care if God came down from the heavens and said: Here's my sperm, free. I'd say: No thanks. Diapers, bottles! I want to be free. You know?"

"Sure," I said.

Suddenly she frowned. "You're not married, are you?"

"No!" I said.

She leaned over and pointed to the ring I wear on my left hand. "What's that ring, then?"

"It's a family crest," I explained. "My father's family comes from Germany."

"It's pretty. . . . Yeah, you look too smart to have gotten hooked this early in life."

"I'm careful," I said, smiling nervously.

She smiled. "Good. Get a good education first. That's what I'm going to do. I'm going to save up from this job and go to New York to college. And then I'm going to get my flying license. I want to be a pilot."

I never heard of a woman pilot. I wonder if she knows what she's doing.

"My uncle's a pilot, so I know how already," she went on. "I can land, I can take off. I just need my license. But it'll be hard. There are still some guys that just won't hire you purely and simply because you're a woman! Isn't that amazing? It's like with my cousin. It's just prejudice. . . . Okay, well, let me know what you decide for your grandparents, okay? What's your name?"

"Spencer."

"Like Tracy? That's cute. I'm Audrey."

After I left the office, I wondered why I hadn't ever seen her at high school if she was my age. There's only one high school for this area, unless you live way at the other side of town. Of course, maybe she wasn't even from around here. Maybe she was just here for a summer job.

I kept thinking about Audrey Rummel throughout the day. She had just a little bit of a Southern accent, like maybe she grew up in Missouri or Texas. I tried to imagine her flying a plane, saying to the passengers: We're approaching the runway now. Why doesn't she just be a flight attendant? They get good money and they get to travel, too. It can't be that hard, just serving people drinks and quieting them down if they get nervous.

I passed by Carnie's house later in the day and showed her the pamphlets I'd picked up. "That's such a nice thought of June's, isn't it?" she said, leafing through them. "She's such a generous person."

"Willa thinks they'll just come home early and won't have a good time," I said. I'd promised to take Carnie to the supermarket. She tore a tendon playing racketball two months ago, and she's still on crutches.

"Oh, Gran'll have a ball," Carnie said. "She loves to dance."

"How about Grandpa?"

"Yeah, well. He'll be okay." She stood up and leaned on me as she slid into the driver's seat. "He can't help being old. We all run down some time."

"I guess."

"All I mean is," she said, making a turn, "you fall in love with a particular person and they come with all kinds of peculiarities that maybe you didn't bargain for. But you handle it, right?"

"Sure," I agreed.

Once we were in the supermarket, I pushed the shopping wagon and got things for Carnie. She only does her shopping once a month, so she gets a whole lot of stuff at one time. While we were by the ice cream section, I saw Taffy. She had her baby in a sling on her back.

"Hi, Spence," she said. "Hi, Mrs. Hayward."

Carnie helps out in the school library some days, so she knows Taffy and Linc and most of my friends. "How's the baby, Taffy?" she asked.

"Oh, he's okay," Taffy said. She didn't look much like a mother in her shorts and T-shirt. She looked over at me. "Remember what I asked you about?"

"What?" I couldn't think what she meant.

"About double-dating. How about Saturday? We're going bowling. Want to come?"

I cleared my throat, remembering the last scene with Linc and Taffy. "Well, I don't know. I'm not dating anyone."

"Should I fix you up?" Taffy asked eagerly. "I know tons of girls who'd like to go out with you."

I knew they were all Taffy's friends from school, the ones who never went out for some good reason or other. "No, I'll find someone."

"My friends are nice!" Taffy sounded indignant.

"Men like to do their own choosing," Carnie said gently.

"Let them! I just thought— He said he didn't have anyone. I was just trying to be helpful." She stared at me balefully. "So call us, okay? It's this Saturday night."

27

After she was out of sight, Carnie winked at me. "Someone's still got a crush on you, kid."

I turned red. "She's—she's married."

Carnie just smiled. "So get me a couple of packages of peas, green beans, and okra. Maybe three of each."

As I went to get them, I thought maybe if I decided to go, I'd ask Audrey Rummel. I wonder if she bowls. She didn't look too athletic, but you can't always tell. Anything'd be better than Taffy dragging along Sharlie Mason or Henrietta Midler.

Carnie bought almost a hundred dollars worth of stuff. I wheeled the cart out to the car and put all the bags in the back. There were ten of them. Then we drove back to her house.

"Let me know how Grandma and Grandpa react," she said.

"I think June wants us to tell them together," I said. "Next Friday when you'll all be coming over for dinner."

I didn't say anything to my grandparents because I figured it was supposed to be a surprise. June and Willa and Carnie and Lizzie talked it over and decided on St. Maarten. All I had to do was go down and get the tickets. June was afraid if it wasn't definite, my grandfather would think of some excuse not to go.

The next day I went down to pay for the tickets. I gave Audrey Rummel the cash in tens, which June had given me, and she wrote it all up. While she was writing, I tried to figure out some way to bring up the subject of going bowling. "Do you, uh, like sports?" I said finally, feeling desperate.

"What ones?" She kept on writing.

28

"Like bowling. I thought you might want to go bowling this Saturday with me and some friends."

"What friends?"

"Some kids I used to hang out with at school. They're married, but they're our age."

She was looking so thoughtful I had the feeling she was going to say no. "I don't know how to bowl," she said.

"Listen, do you want to come or what?" I hate it when girls do that, prolonging the agony like they were enjoying keeping you guessing.

"Sure, I'll come. Here's my address." She smiled and wrote it down on a piece of paper. "Actually I'm twenty," she said, handing it to me. "I've been out of school two years. Is that okay?"

"Sure." She did look a little older, more sophisticated than most of the girls I know.

"Some guys get a heart attack if you're older."

"I'm flexible," I said.

Audrey laughed. "I don't want to embarrass you in front of your friends. I'm a klutz at most sports."

"You won't embarrass me." I was more afraid she'd think Taffy and Linc were jerks. I took the tickets and put them in my pocket. "So, I'll see you Saturday, okay?" I said.

As I was walking out, a man walked in and started asking her about his vacation plans. I stopped just outside the door to watch her talk to him. Now that I knew she was older, she looked older, but not in a bad way. I felt terrific that she'd said yes.

# 4

When she saw the tickets to St. Maarten, my grandmother burst into tears. That got my grandfather angry. "What're you getting her upset about?" he said. "This is a party."

"It's a surprise," June said to him, talking loud and clear. "For your anniversary. We're sending you and Gran on a trip."

"A trip? What kind of trip?"

"To a beautiful place, with sand and ocean. You can lie in the sun, gather sea shells . . ."

My grandfather looked disgusted. "Sea shells? I'm not going on any damn fool trip to collect sea shells."

"See, Gran." Willa was showing her the pamphlet, which had photos of the island. "You can go dancing. It's a beautiful hotel. Your room has a terrace."

My grandmother was sniffling, but with pleasure. "What girls! What girls I have! To think of something like this!"

"I'm not going," my grandfather said, "and that's

31

that. You didn't even ask. What kind of surprise is that?"

"Grandpa," Carnie said patiently. "It wouldn't have been a surprise if you'd known ahead of time. It's only for two weeks. Everything'll be taken care of. You won't have to do a thing except relax and enjoy yourself."

"I can do that right here." He glared at me. "Let *him* go. *He* likes to relax. That's all he ever does." My grandfather basically thinks I'm a bum.

Willa took him by the shoulders. "This is for *you*, for you and Gran. It's for your anniversary. You've been married fifty years."

"I know how long I've been married! I'm not senile yet."

"Gran wants to go, don't you, Gran?" June asked softly.

A few tears were still trickling down my grandmother's cheeks. "Of course," she said.

"Let her go by herself," he said. "If she wants to go, let her go. I'm not stopping her."

Lizzie let out a huff. "Grandpa, what is *wrong* with you? You're a selfish rude old beast sometimes. You'll have fun!"

"I don't *want* to have fun," my grandfather said. "I've *had* fun. I've had all the fun I want."

"Do if for Gran, then. It'll make her happy."

My grandfather looked at my grandmother. "Is that what it takes to make you happy?" he said.

"I'd like to go," my grandmother said hesitantly.

He began looking at the pamphlets. "How much will all this come to?"

"It's all paid for," Carnie said.

"I want to know what I'm getting for my money.

Maybe it's some racket, some gyp. You get there and there's no hot water. It's just a lot of natives running around cheating you, selling you stuff you don't need."

Willa rolled her eyes. "Is taking a vacation, a free, entirely paid-for vacation such a terrible thing?"

"It's a terrible thing to waste money," he said. "You don't know. I lived through the Depression."

If I had a dollar for every talk I've had to listen to by my grandfather about the Depression, I'd be richer than Rockefeller. "June saved the money," I said.

"How?" He looked suddenly suspicious. "You didn't take it from that fellow, did you?"

"What fellow?" June said.

"You know who I mean. That no-good." He always refers to Silas that way.

June looked like she was going to cry. "Daddy, we've been divorced for two years. And he's *not* a no-good."

"He made you unhappy," my grandmother said. She always gets nervous if Silas is mentioned. "That's all he means."

Carnie took my grandmother's hand. "So, it's all settled, right? You'll go, you'll have a wonderful time."

"*She'll* have a wonderful time," my grandfather said. "*I'm* not having any wonderful time."

"Okay, you'll have a rotten time," Lizzie exploded. "Okay? You'll stew in your own juices."

My grandfather looked at her with a half smile. "You think I'm a selfish old beast, huh?"

She laughed. "Only some of the time."

"I am. I'm a selfish old beast. You reach my age and you can be whatever kind of beast you want."

33

June came over and kissed his forehead. "You're not a beast," she crooned.

"*He* thinks I am," he said, looking at me. "Don't you?"

I wish I had the nerve to talk back to my grandfather the way Lizzie does. But I still live at home, and anyway, it never seems worth it. I just shrugged.

One thing I know: If it was my money, I wouldn't spend it on him, that's for sure.

"I haven't danced in so long," my grandmother said dreamily. "I used to be so good."

"Put on some music," Carnie said. "Get something on the radio, Spence."

I found a station that had dance music. I went over to my grandmother. "Want to dance, lady?"

She turned pink. "Lady! Sure, I want to." She put her arms up and we danced. Lizzie danced with June while Carnie, Willa, and my grandfather watched. My grandmother is a little plump, but she's still a good dancer. When we were done, Carnie applauded.

"Two women, dancing," my grandfather said. "What is that? Some new fad?"

"No, we're gay, Grandpa," Lizzie said. "We're running off together."

He scowled. "What kind of joke is that? That's nothing to joke about!"

"You're still a good dancer, Gran," I told her. I danced with Willa and June while Carnie and Lizzie went into the kitchen to get some soft drinks.

"This is turning into some kind of dance hall," my grandfather said. "All these women."

Lizzie tried to lug him to his feet. "Come on, you dance, too."

"Leave me alone. I'm too old."

"You're not! You're young at heart. Come on."
She'd gotten him to his feet. Suddenly he began to
dance, some weird little dance that didn't have
anything to do with the music.

"See," June said. "You can do it."

He raised his hands up as though he were clicking
castanets. "The dance of the selfish old beast," he
said.

Willa winked at my grandmother. "You better look
out, Gran. Some lady's going to steal him away if
you're not careful."

My grandfather was still dancing around, doing this
peculiar little step. "I'm in my prime," he said.
"Years of experience. You can't beat that."

My grandmother was looking anxious. "Don't
overdo, dear."

He was puffing, but he kept on. "You're the one
who got me going. Now I can't stop."

I went over and turned the dance music off. My
grandfather glared at me. "Party pooper," he said
angrily, sitting down again.

"He's concerned with your health," my grandmother said. "Even though you're in wonderful
shape."

Sometimes it seems like my grandfather has a
harem, what with all my sisters and my grandmother
buzzing around him. Whether they're scolding him or
petting him, they act like he's some king who has all
the answers. And you can tell he gets a big bang out of
it, even though he grumbles and claims they're ruining
his life and says all he wants to do is sit in a corner and
sleep. Now he sat in his favorite rocker and looked at
me suspiciously. It's as though from time to time my
grandfather becomes aware of my existence and then

goes back to forgetting about it. "So, what are you doing with yourself these days, Spencer? College start yet?"

"Not till fall." I never know with him if he's really that senile or forgetful, or if he just forgets some things to get me mad. Anyone knows college starts in the fall.

"Got a job? All your sisters are working. What are you up to?"

"Yeah, I've got a job."

Carnie handed me a soft drink in a tall orange glass with ice. "He helps Mercer sometimes," she said.

"He's working at the hospital, dear," my grandmother said. "You know that."

"No, I don't know that," my grandfather said irritably. "How should I know? No one ever tells me anything. What's he doing at the hospital? He's not a doctor, is he?"

"I'm a donor," I said.

My grandfather screwed up his face. "A what?"

"I'm a donor at a sperm bank."

"A bank? What kind of bank?"

"It's a new clinic," Willa intervened swiftly. "For women who have trouble conceiving, Grandpa. This is a way of helping them so they can have children."

"A bank?" my grandfather repeated. "You give them money so they can buy a baby, is that it? Is this legal?"

I get so tense when I talk to my grandfather that it's lucky I have low blood pressure. Otherwise I might just kill him. "I donate my sperm," I said, "and the doctors do the injecting. Then the women get pregnant, so it's their baby. They're the mother and I'm the father."

36

My grandfather looked around at all my sisters. "*He's* a father? At his age? What are you, sixteen, seventeen?"

"Eighteen," I said.

"It's symbolic," Carnie said. "He's not the father in the sense of having to raise the child. He just helps create it."

"So, who's raising these kids?" my grandfather said. "He's impregnating all these women and that's it? *That's* a job?"

My grandmother was sitting at my grandfather's side. "You see, dear, there are women who have trouble conceiving. This way they have options other than adopting."

"What's wrong with adopting?" he wanted to know.

"Nothing's wrong with it, Grandpa," Carnie said, "but remember all the trouble I've had with the adoption agency? There aren't that many kids to go around."

"I'm just helping them," I said, trying to sound calm and patient. "It's just an act of human kindness . . . like giving blood. They screen you. They don't pick just anyone. You have to have good genes, be in good shape. It's an honor to be chosen."

"It *is* an honor," my grandmother chimed in. "I feel proud of Spencer. Dear, don't you remember how agonizing it was for me, when we were trying?" She looked flustered and trailed off.

"What was agonizing about it?" my grandfather said.

Tears came to my grandmother's eyes. "The day Eleanor was born was the happiest day of my life."

Eleanor was my mother, my grandmother's only

child. She still keeps her photo on her bureau. She was pretty, more like Carnie and Lizzie than Willa and June—dark-haired, with big soft brown eyes. My father was a lot taller than her—six-two, like me. I think I get my aptitude for sports from him. Usually I don't miss my parents. How could I, since I never knew them? But sometimes I get angry, thinking of how different my life could've been if that stupid drunk driver hadn't plowed into them that night. That's one thing I'll never do—drink and drive. I think they ought to take those guys and run them over. Instead they get six months' suspension on their license or something.

Everyone was silent as they always are when my mother is mentioned. Even my grandfather looked grim, like it'd happened yesterday.

Then June opened a map on the table. "Anyway, we're here because you both made it through fifty years, and now, as a reward, you're going to have a super vacation."

My grandfather looked down at the map. "Are we flying to this godforsaken place?"

"It's all paid for," June said. "You'll be flying Friday night, July 25th."

"Well," my grandfather said. "It looks like you women have everything all decided, as usual. That's the way it always is." He winked at me. "They decide, we comply. The law of the jungle."

"Grandpa, you're really impossible," Lizzie said. She went over and hugged me and whispered in my ear, "Don't mind him."

"In *my* day," he said, "if you went out and impregnated lots of women you didn't know, they went after you with a shotgun. They didn't *pay* you."

38

I decided to try one more time. "Grandpa, I'm not having sex with them. Don't you understand? I don't even *see* them."

"It was better the old way," he said. "What's the point if you don't even see them?"

I let them sit around and talk some more about the vacation. I went up to my room.

You can't explain *anything* to my grandfather. It's not just this. He's that way about everything. Tell him something, and the next day he's got it all twisted around. Sometimes it seems like his whole aim in life is driving people crazy. Just to take my mind off it, I called Linc and told him I could go bowling with them on Saturday. "Tell Taffy not to bother getting someone for me," I said. "I asked someone."

"Yeah, who?" he asked eagerly. Since he got married, Linc's really interested in everyone's sex life.

"Her name's Audrey. I don't know her that well. I just met her."

He laughed. "Can she bowl?"

"Pretty much. You'll see."

"It'll be like old times, huh?" he said.

"Right," I said. I guess he meant like before they were married.

5

The bowling alley we always went to in high school is called Veronica's. Veronica is a big fat lady who used to be some kind of bowling champ. She can still roll them pretty good, but mostly she sits at the bar and gets people drinks. Our crowd always liked her because she wasn't that fussy about your age in terms of serving whatever you felt like. If you got really pissed, she pitched you, but otherwise she was good-natured.

Audrey looked nice. She had on tight faded jeans, a red shirt knotted at the waist, and a gold chain around her neck. She was wearing big round glasses, but they didn't make her look any less pretty. "I have these new contacts," she said, "but they were bothering me."

We played a few rounds, but Audrey was right; she was terrible. Some people catch on right away, and you can tell if they kept at it, they'd be good. Other people just don't seem to know how to do it. "I told you," she said, laughing. "I'm hopeless."

Then she sat down with Taffy and let Linc and me play by ourselves for a while.

"Not bad," Linc said, under his breath. "You just met her?"

When we sat down for a beer, Taffy began questioning her. "Did you go to Riverview? I never saw you."

Audrey was smoking. She blew some smoke out and waved it away with her hand. She has long nails. "I moved here with my mother after high school. I've been out two years now."

"Are you going to college?" Taffy asked.

"I was. . . . But I dropped out to get married. I'm divorced now."

There was a slight pause.

"You're divorced already?" Linc said, looking slightly alarmed.

"Yeah, it only lasted a year and a half. We had, like, different goals," Audrey said. "He had this fantasy that I was supposed to be some happy little housewife catering to his needs, you know, the whole Neanderthal thing. And I just said: Shove it . . . I'm going to be a pilot."

"Of an airplane?" Taffy said.

Linc looked at her in disgust. "No, of an elephant," he said.

"You mean, you're going to actually *fly* the plane?" Taffy pursued, her eyes round. "Don't you need a license?"

"Oh, yeah," Audrey said, chain-lighting another cigarette. "I have a ways to go. Even after you get your license, you need four thousand hours of flying time before you can get any kind of decent job. But I'll hang in there. I have a lot of endurance."

Taffy gulped down some beer. "So, you kind of gave up on your marriage?"

Audrey shrugged. "It just gave out, that's all. Like I said, we just looked at everything differently. He wanted kids, the whole bit."

"What's wrong with that?" Linc said indignantly.

"Nothing . . . just not for me. I'm not the maternal type. Oh, listen, for other people, they're fine."

"We have a baby," Taffy said nervously. She rooted around in her purse and got out a photo. "His name is Webster."

Audrey looked at the photo. "Cute," she said dismissively. She handed the photo to me. "They have a baby."

"I know," I said.

"We all went to high school together," Taffy said. "I used to go out with Spence in junior high. We're all really good friends."

Audrey handed her back the photo. "I didn't mean anything personal against babies," she said. "Someone's got to have them or the world would grind to a halt, right? But I figure you're only young once."

"I'm going to college," Taffy said defensively. "Once Web's in school. I agree with you. I want to do something, too."

"Like what?" Linc said sarcastically. "Fly a plane?"

Taffy turned red. "You don't have any faith in me," she whispered. "There's lots of things I can do."

"My husband was like that," Audrey said, "and it got me really pissed. But then I thought, why argue? It's his hangup. I'll have faith in myself. That's what counts—having faith in yourself."

Linc was looking at me, like: Where did you find

her? I kept looking at Taffy, who was sitting there miserably, bending the edge of the photo back and forth, looking like she was about to cry.

"Do you have faith in me, Spence?" Taffy asked suddenly, her voice shaking.

"Sure," I said uneasily.

"I got all As in junior year," she rambled on, looking from me to Audrey. "I just didn't do that well senior year because I was so, because of, because I got pregnant." Then she started to cry.

I felt really awkward about the whole scene. I just sat there and looked at Linc, who looked awkward, too. But Audrey put her arm around Taffy like they'd known each other a long time. "I was like that, too," she said. "But you'll be okay. The baby'll be in school, you'll go back. My mom did that."

Taffy was still sniffing. "I'm not even good with him," she said. "I'm not even a good mother."

"Yeah, you're good with him," Linc said. He looked at me. "Don't you think she is, Spence?"

"Sure," I agreed quickly. "You're good, Taffy."

After that Taffy and Audrey went off to the ladies room and Linc and I bowled some more. At midnight Linc said they should get back because the baby sometimes woke up for his feeding.

I'd borrowed our family car. I drove Audrey back to her house. I didn't know exactly what to expect from her. She'd been married, divorced. All that made her seem older, even though she really wasn't much older than me. She didn't seem the type you'd make out with in a car. I turned the motor off and we just sat there. It was a hot night. I hoped I hadn't gotten too sweaty bowling.

"Those poor kids," Audrey said. She said it the

way my grandmother might, like they were another generation almost.

"Taffy's sort of emotional," I explained.

"Was she your girlfriend?" She lit up another cigarette.

"Just for a little while, in junior high."

"I had the feeling she was kind of sizing me up." I hesitated. "You know, you shouldn't smoke so much."

"Yeah, I know. I have a lot of bad habits." Then she turned and smiled at me. "Do you?"

"What?" I wanted to kiss her, but wasn't sure how to begin.

"Tell me about your bad habits," Audrey said, moving closer.

"I don't have any," I admitted. "I stay in good shape, I run, I eat properly . . ."

"How about girls?"

"I like girls." That sounded dumb, but I went on, "I—I like you."

"So kiss me, okay?"

I pulled her into my arms and brought my mouth down on hers. About five minutes later we came up for air. It's funny how with kissing, which seems a fairly simple thing, so much else is going on. Some girls seem to be fighting some inward battle even while it's happening, like they're worrying about what might happen next. It's like they have some mental brakes on all the time. But with Audrey it was the opposite. She just kind of melted into me, and I felt like I could have done just about anything I wanted. She reached up and ran her fingers through my hair. I have curly hair that I try to remember to cut every once in a while. It's pretty long now.

"I love your hair," she said, sighing. "You look like an angel."

I laughed. My thoughts at that moment weren't that angelic.

"Those blue eyes. My first boyfriend had blue eyes. I'm kind of a sucker for them." She glanced around at the back of the car. It's kind of messy. "You want to know something strange?" she said. "I've never done it in a car. Do you think that's un-American? The reason is, I never really dated all that much in high school, and then, when I was a junior, I met my husband and he was ten years older. He had his own apartment. I guess I wanted to grow up fast, skip all that stuff, that awkward fumbling with guys my own age."

I've done my share of awkward fumbling. "What did your husband do?"

"He's into computers. He used to sell lumber in Maine, but he got tired of it." She reached into her purse and pulled out a photo of herself with him. He was short, with glasses, not much taller than her.

I handed the photo back to her. "Why did you get divorced?" I asked.

She sighed. "He was just too old or I was too young, or something."

A minute later we started kissing again. This time when we broke apart, Audrey gave a kind of strangled laugh. "I'd ask you in, only my mom is up." She glanced toward the back seat again. "I don't have anything against cars."

"I—I don't have any protection," I stammered.

"That's okay. I have an IUD. I don't get any side effects and my doctor says it's safe."

46

"Yeah, well." I didn't want to hurt her feelings. "I don't know."

"What don't you know?"

I tried to figure out how to put it. "I have this job that . . . I'm not supposed to have sex with anyone."

Audrey looked at me in surprise. "What kind of job is that?"

I told her.

"I don't get it," she said. "Why can't you do it between times?"

"It might lower my sperm count." I cleared my throat. "That's one reason they chose me, because I have a high count."

"What a terrible job to have!" She looked horrified.

"No, it's an honor. I'm glad to have it. They only pick one out of five who apply."

"I guess I just feel really disappointed. You mean, all we can have is a platonic relationship?"

She looked so depressed, I reached out and touched her. "Well, we can . . . do other things."

"Jesus." Audrey took out another cigarette. "Ever since that day in the office, I've been imagining . . . Listen, why don't you quit the job? Do they pay you a whole lot?"

"I'm not doing it for the money," I said. "You go through all these tests. They'd really be mad if I quit now."

She blew out a stream of smoke. "I once read in the average ejaculation there's nine quadrillion sperm. You'd have plenty left."

"It's not just that." I knew I wasn't being exactly truthful.

Audrey looked at me with her big, soft hazel eyes.

"Did you have some kind of bad experience with girls, Spence?"

"No, I . . . no. Actually, I've never . . . I mean, I've had experience with girls, but I've never actually done the whole thing." I felt like a real jerk admitting that. "I think you're a very nice person," I added, afraid I might hurt her feelings. "I'd like to go out with you more, if you still want."

Audrey was staring pensively out the window. "Sure, we can go out." She sighed. "When I think of all the guys who would've leapt at this chance! And here I fall for someone who doesn't even find me tempting."

I pulled her over toward me. "I *do* find you tempting," I said. "Very."

"Do you really?"

"Sure."

"So, you're not just using this an excuse?"

"Definitely not."

We sat there together with our arms around each other. "Okay," Audrey said. "I'm glad you at least . . . I mean, now I know. And we can still mingle our souls, if not our bodies, right?"

"Yeah, right."

I watched her walk into the house, her ass moving sexily in her jeans. She has this funny mixture of seeming tough at times, like with her smoking, and then suddenly saying these poetical things like about mingling our souls. I like that.

6

Taffy called the next morning to apologize for crying. At least that's why she said she called. "Are you really going out with that girl, Audrey?"

"Yeah," I said. It was eleven in the morning, but I hadn't even had breakfast yet. My mouth felt all fuzzy.

"She seemed sort of hard to me," Taffy said stiffly. "She didn't seem like your type, Spence. Where'd you meet her?"

"At a travel agency."

"Well, I know it's none of my business," Taffy said, "but I just think I should warn you. I bet anything she'll try to seduce you. She seemed like the type that's mainly after sex."

"I don't think so."

"You could have your choice of just about anyone you wanted," she said, "so I hate to see you throw yourself away on just anyone. Especially someone older who smoked all the time."

"Okay," I said, beginning to feel annoyed. "I won't bring her if we double again."

"Oh, no, bring her," Taffy said. "Actually, it was Linc who said she didn't seem like your type, not even liking babies. It was him."

After I hung up, I took a long hot shower. I knew Taffy was just jealous of Audrey. I guess I can't blame her, but she's married now, with a kid. Shouldn't she be concentrating on that?

Maybe Audrey isn't my type, but so what? I'm not going to marry her. She just seems like a nice, interesting, unusual person. Maybe I'll be a good influence on her and get her to give up smoking. Some people want to stop, but don't have the incentive.

When I got downstairs, my grandmother was in the kitchen reading the pamphlets about their trip. I gave her a hug. "I'm so excited," she said. "Look at this pool, Spence! Oh, I wish you could come. You're such a good swimmer. You'd have a wonderful time."

"I wish I could, too," I admitted.

"I'm not even sure Omar will enjoy himself," she said. "He can be so stubborn."

"He'll probably have a ball," I said.

I was being sarcastic, but my grandmother said eagerly, "Do you really think so? That's what I hope. If I can just get him there. You know the funny thing? He was such a playful man when I first met him. Always telling jokes, loved to dance. Suddenly in the last bunch of years, it seems like the steam's gone out of him. Oh, maybe it's my fault. Maybe I go at him too much."

"No, you don't," I said. "He's just an old guy . . . and you're—well, young at heart."

My grandmother dyes her hair blond and she's put

on a bit of weight, but she struck a glamour girl pose. "Young at heart," she said. Then she looked glum again. "I did everything so young. You young people today are smart, delaying things, thinking things over."

I wonder how my grandmother would like Audrey. Maybe I'll bring her around sometime. My grandmother's usually pretty good. It's my grandfather who often makes some weird sarcastic remark the next day, like, "How come her teeth were crooked?" or "How come she has a Polish name?"

I had promised Mercer I'd help him out on a carpentry job that afternoon. I still prefer it if he sends someone to help me, but if he doesn't, I can usually manage on my own.

The woman whose house I went to looked angry the minute I arrived. "It's two o'clock," she said.

"Yeah, right." My arm hurt from lugging the toolbox. It weighed around thirty pounds.

"They said they'd have someone here at noon on the dot! I can't wait around and wait around."

I shrugged. "Lady, they told me two. I'm sorry."

"I hope you at least have the proper equipment. The last man they sent didn't even come equipped with what he needed."

I brought in the toolbox that has most of the stuff I need for these jobs, and I went into the kitchen to look at what needed to be done. The other guy had left things in kind of a mess—wires sticking out of the wall, plaster on the floor. "What exactly remains to be done?" I asked.

She explained what she wanted: A new light had been put up over her sink, and a ceiling fixture near the back door. The electrical work was finished; I just needed to plaster and paint over it so it would blend in, then put wallpaper over that. "But I'm warning you, I have an appointment at four. Are you a fast worker?"

"Yes, ma'am."

"Fast *and* efficient?"

"Right."

I think it was her coming in every fifteen minutes to see how I was doing that got me spooked. "Can you give me an estimate of approximately when you'll be done?" she asked. I was up on the ladder, which wasn't all that steady.

"Pretty soon," I said.

"How soon is pretty soon?"

I glanced at her kitchen clock. It was three-twenty. "By four, I think."

"You think! The other man was here four hours, you're here two. . . . And you look extremely young to me. How long have you worked for this firm?"

I was perspiring like crazy. "Two years," I lied.

"Two *years*? Then you've had considerable experience?"

"Yes, ma'am."

At ten of four she looked in again. "Well?" was all she said.

"I—I think it may take a little longer than I thought," I said.

The woman struck her brow. "You can tell your boss that this is the last time I'm using his firm *ever*."

"Okay," I said. "I'll tell him."

Her arms were crossed. "What am I going to do? I have an appointment!"

"I can just keep on working," I said. "You go."

"Can I trust you alone in the house? Are you a trustworthy person?"

I was really pissed, but I just said, "Yeah, I'm trustworthy."

"Well, I don't really have a choice, do I? If Janice comes home—well, I'll leave a note for her so she won't be terrified if she comes into the kitchen."

I didn't ask her who Janice was. I just kept on working, even after the door slammed. About half an hour after she left, I called Mercer.

"How's it going?" he asked. He's always in the middle of a dozen things.

"It's going to take another hour or two at least. The lady's really mad."

"Have you got all the stuff you need?"

"Uh-huh."

"Just keep at it. Don't let her bug you."

Actually, I worked better with the lady gone. I was filthy and sweaty, but at least I could concentrate. About half an hour later a girl walked into the kitchen. She was tall and skinny, with red hair, and looked about my age. "Hi, I'm Janice," she said, opening the refrigerator door. "Are you the carpenter?"

"Yeah."

"Boy, it's hot in here! Want a beer?" She had taken two cans out of the refrigerator.

I looked longingly at the beer. I knew how good it would taste. "I'm not supposed to drink on the job," I said slowly, tempted.

"Oh, come on. On a day like this?" She snapped the top off one can and handed it to me, then snapped one off for herself. She took a long sip of the beer. "Boy, I love beer," she said. "Beer and piña coladas. I

53

could drink them all day. Are you the same guy who was here yesterday? Mom was ready to kill him."

"No, I'm someone else." I climbed down off the ladder. "She's going to kill me if she comes back and finds I'm not finished with the job."

Janice was staring at me appraisingly. "Yeah, she'll kill you, all right."

We finished our beers. "See you," she called, strolling out of the door.

The lady came back about twenty minutes later. Luckily, I was still working, though I hadn't gotten very far. "What *is* all this?" she said. "You're not done yet?"

"I'm almost done," I said.

Suddenly her eyes lit on the beer cans which Janice had forgotten to toss out. "Have you been drinking on the job?"

"No, ma'am, your daughter came home."

"What is *wrong* with Janice? Did she offer you a beer too?"

I swallowed. "Just a sip."

"That girl is on the road to being an alcoholic, and she thinks I don't notice! I count how many cans are in the fridge, and she—" She narrowed her eyes.

I watched her toss the empty beer cans contemptuously into the garbage.

Janice returned a few minutes later, and her mother started screaming at her awhile about the beer. While her mother was screaming, Janice was smiling up at me. "Stop it, Janice!" her mother said. "That's a workman, and he's trying to do his job. You're distracting him."

"I think I'm almost finished," I said. "Could, uh,

one of you hand me the fixture?" I'd wanted to finish the wallpaper before I screwed the fixture in.

The woman handed me a round white globe, which I fit on as best I could. She turned it on and it worked. "Well, finally!" she said. "Glory hallelujah."

I swept up the mess in the kitchen and started getting ready to go. "Ma'am, can I use your bathroom?" I asked her.

She pointed out where it was. I washed my face and neck, as much for the coolness of the water as for making myself look decent. I had to check in with Mercer before I went home. It was almost six. Just as I was walking down the hall, I heard a crash. I walked into the kitchen. The fixture had fallen to the floor and smashed into thousands of tiny pieces.

"Oh good Christ," the woman said. "Janice, don't go *in* there! You'll get glass in your feet." She turned to me in fury. "What does this mean?"

I shrugged. "I guess it just fell."

"Young man." She moved closer to me. "That fixture cost fifty dollars. Are you going to go out and with your own personal money purchase me another exactly like it?"

"I've got to talk to my boss," I said, feeling my stomach churn.

"You do that. . . . You've been here four hours, and all I have to show for it is a broken piece of glass. And you've been drinking on the job."

"He was just thirsty, Mom," Janice put in. "He was just keeping me company."

"Then why don't *you* save up your allowance money and buy a new fixture?" she said to her daughter. "Will you do that, Miss Beer Head?"

Janice giggled.

I started out. I really wasn't sure what had happened. The fixture had seemed to fit on fine. Maybe I should've tested it myself. Maybe the cord didn't have enough give. But really, it's the electrician's fault. That part of it was his responsibility.

Mercer is usually a good guy, basically laid back, genial, even though he says that in his business, which he runs himself, there are a hundred crises a minute. I was surprised that when I walked in his door, his first words were, "Spencer, what in God's name have you been up to?"

His office was air-conditioned. It really felt good. Outside it must have been ninety-five at least. "The thing is, the fixture just fell," I said. "All I did was go in to wash up, and whammo, there it was on the floor. Maybe it was defective or something."

His phone started ringing. Without answering it, he jabbed a button and it stopped. "This lady is threatening to sue me. Now she won't. I know that type, but you were there four hours, the job was half done. Did you check when you were up there to make sure it fit tightly? How *could* it just slip off?"

"I wasn't even there when it happened," I said.

He sighed. "She says you were drinking on the job and making eyes at her daughter. How about that part of it?"

"Look, Merc, it was a really hot day. Her daughter came home and offered me a beer. I was thirsty. Is that such a crime?"

"You just drank the beer and that was that? No hanky-panky while the mother was gone and you were supposed to be working?"

I felt hurt. "I wouldn't do that . . . I just met her."

"Look, Spence, my reputation is on the line every time I send someone out. You can't make mistakes. This lady thinks you're a union member who's been with me two years. Now I'm going to have to send someone back who really is, and that'll cost me."

"I can go back," I offered.

He laughed. "Please. I don't want to go out of business. You just go home and take a shower. You look like a mess."

I looked at him. "But you will still give me work? I need it. I really need to save money for college. And I did the plastering and the wallpapering fine. Really."

Mercer got up and slapped me on the back. "I'll give you work. I'll probably live to regret it, but I will. Now will you promise me never to accept anything alcoholic on the job and to stay out of trouble with girls, no matter how fetchingly they come on to you?"

"I didn't *do* anything with her!" I sighed. "I've got a girlfriend. I wouldn't do that."

"Who's that?" Mercer asked, seeing me out. "Anyone we know?"

"Uh-uh. I met her at the travel agency when I went to get the tickets for Grandma and Grandpa."

"Bring her around sometime. We'd like to meet her."

Even though Mercer said he'd still give me work, I felt worried as I drove home. Worried and angry, too. First at that dumb Janice for horsing around. Maybe she did get me flustered and that was why the fixture fell. But I was amazed that Mercer thought I was the kind of person who'd just start making out with someone I didn't even know right on the job, like I don't have any sense of values. I won the senior class

57

essay on "The Values That Have Guided Me Throughout Life." He acts like I'm some kind of jerk.

"Did you have a hard day, dear?" my grandmother asked at dinner. We eat early, at five-thirty, so I'd just had time to shower; my hair was still wet.

"It was okay," I said, not wanting to go into it.

"How many ladies did you knock up today?" my grandfather asked, winking at me.

I didn't reply.

"Well? Let us know. We're too old to go to porno movies. We need a little excitement."

My grandmother glared at him. "Omar, stop that! You know Spencer is doing this as a community service. Please stop putting smutty implications into it."

"Today I was working for Mercer," I said, reaching for seconds on meat loaf.

"What's he doing getting involved in this?" my grandfather said. "I thought he ran a construction business."

"He does," I said, imagining dumping the whole bowl of mashed potatoes over his head. "That's what I was helping him with. I was plastering and doing wallpaper for some lady's kitchen." I spoke clearly and distinctly, like he was an idiot.

"A busy lad," my grandfather said, wolfing in his potatoes.

"You should relax, too," my grandmother urged. "You mustn't work *too* hard, hon."

"Oh, I don't," I said. "I'm going out on Friday."

"Who with?" She looked pleased. "One of your nice girlfriends from school?"

"No, her name's Audrey Rummel. She graduated two years ago. She's—um—divorced."

"Divorced?" my grandfather said, like he'd never heard of that. "You're going out with a divorced woman at your age?"

"She's my age," I said, clenching my fists under the table. "She just married young and it didn't work out."

"And she hasn't learned her lesson? Now she's after you? She wrecked one man's life and now she's looking for another—"

"Does she have any children?" my grandmother broke in nervously.

I shook my head.

"Well, there you are!" my grandmother said to my grandfather. "It's just as if she was never married then. Just a youthful indiscretion. That happens to many perfectly lovely young girls."

He snorted. Then he pointed a finger at me. "You watch out, young man. Those divorcées are just after one thing. I'm just giving you a piece of friendly advice."

"Spencer *knows* all that," my grandmother said firmly, getting up to clear. "He can take care of himself."

Sometimes I try to imagine my grandfather actually coming around courting my grandmother, bringing her flowers, taking her nice places for dinner, kissing her goodnight, trying to get her to like him. Because my grandmother's a nice person. I can't imagine her marrying someone with a personality like my grandfather's is now. She'd have to be totally crazy to do that. Anyone would.

I picked Audrey up at her house Friday. She said her mother was upstairs. "You'll meet her next time," she said. "She's getting ready to go off for the weekend."

"Where's she going?" I asked. Audrey looked beautiful. She had on a white dress with a full skirt and some kind of terrific perfume.

"She has a boyfriend." Audrey slid into the car next to me. "Only he's in the middle of one of these long, agonizing divorces, so—"

"What happened to your father?" I started the car up.

"He took off, you know, the way some men do. We never heard from him again. . . . Spence?"

"Yeah?"

"Would it, like, hurt your pride at all if we took my car? It's a little newer, and I thought it might be more comfortable."

"No, I don't mind," I said. I wish I had money to get a new great car of my own. That's the first thing

I'm going to do if I can save the money. Audrey has a Honda. It was nice, with soft bucket seats.

"It was a farewell present from my husband," she explained, giving me the keys.

"That was really nice of him," I said. "If you got divorced and all."

"Oh, he's a nice guy," Audrey said. "We're still friends."

I started up the car. It drove smoothly.

"I thought maybe later we could go back," Audrey said. "We'll have the whole house to ourselves. She won't be back till Monday."

My heart started thumping. The few times I'd even been alone in a house with a girl, her parents were always out playing bridge or something, and you knew they might come home any second. Emmy Lou and I used to go down to the den in her basement, but once her father, who happened to be my history teacher, came home unexpectedly because he wasn't feeling well and turned on the lights. Luckily—this was pure luck, because maybe I wouldn't have graduated otherwise—he didn't see us. We were sunk so far down on the couch that he just clicked the lights off again and went on upstairs.

There isn't much choice if you want to see a movie in our town. There are two movie theaters, and they keep running the same features for months. We went into one about a girl who was murdered. It was kind of gory. They kept flashing back to the gory parts all through it. About halfway through Audrey whispered to me, "Hey, let's go, okay?"

I never walk out of movies, no matter how bad they are. I figure I've paid my money and maybe the end will be good. But I followed her on out. "Ugh," she said, shivering. "I hate movies like that!"

"You mean, because of the violence?"

She was walking fast, her heels clicking down the street. "No, because every Hollywood movie I see is the same *crap*! Some dopey passive blond with big boobs gets shafted by men. So what else is new?"

I wasn't sure what to say. The movie hadn't seemed that good to me, but it seemed realistic. "It shows what life is really like," I said.

"Why didn't she have a sister," Audrey asked, "a skinny, flat-chested smart girl who ends up with a great boyfriend who treats her wonderfully *and* she gets a good job and doesn't take shit from anybody? That's real life, too."

"Sure," I said. "That would be good, too."

Actually, Audrey has pretty large-sized breasts, so it didn't seem like she'd be that sensitive on the subject. I tried not to look at them. "There's more to women than tits," she fumed. "That's the least of us. I wish they'd do some operation on all the women in the world so they wouldn't have them anymore if all they do is make men act like insane nincompoops."

"But then how would babies get, you know, stuff to drink?" It didn't sound like a good idea to me.

"Bottles!"

If I were a baby, I think I'd prefer a breast. It at least gives them something soft and nice to hang on to while they're drinking. But I shut up and concentrated on driving us back to her house.

Audrey's house was dark when we got back there. She went around flipping on a lot of lights. "It always looks spooky to me when it's dark," she said. "Especially after seeing a movie like that. I hate staying here alone when Mom's gone. Even though we have nine million locks."

"I'll take care of you," I said, though if someone came in with a gun, I don't know. I'd probably run and hide.

Audrey had a nice room, not that different from the rooms of some girls I went out with in high school except her bed was bigger and she didn't have a lot of stuffed animals all over it. There was just the bed and a bureau with a few big pillows on the floor. She went to the bureau and squirted some perfume on herself. "That was Mike's favorite," she said. "Charlie. Do you like it?"

I nodded. I wasn't sure how to proceed. Audrey was standing across the room with her shoes off, then she walked over and put her arms around my waist. She kissed my chin. "Should I take my clothes off or do you want to?" she asked softly.

I turned red. No one ever put it quite that bluntly before. "Uh—whatever," I said.

Then without saying anything else, she just took her clothes off! She draped them over the chair, not even looking at me. Maybe she was expecting I'd do the same, because when she looked up and saw me still standing there in kind of a daze, she said, "Are you okay?"

"Sure," I said.

Audrey walked over toward me, naked. She looked beautiful. I guess not all women look beautiful without their clothes, or maybe it's that after a while you get blasé about everything they have, but I haven't reached that stage yet. I still find it all kind of amazing. I took my clothes off in a hurry then and we lay down on her bed. It all seemed frighteningly easy.

We were there in the house alone, in bed, no clothes. I'm used to spending all my time figuring out how to deal with all the barriers—the girl's inhibitions, her parents, my wondering if she'd hate it. To tell the truth, I've never been with a girl who'd actually done it, not that I knew of, anyway. Some girls at our school probably had but wouldn't have told.

I don't know if it was any of those things, but I couldn't get hard. I felt excited, but it didn't seem to go from my head to down below, even though Audrey was kissing me and caressing me and doing everything she could to put me in the mood. "Some guys don't like it if you show you're available," she said, pulling back finally. "Is that it?"

"No . . . it's more what I said that other time."

"What? I don't remember."

"Well, because of my job and all . . . I feel like maybe I ought to save myself for that."

"Spence, come on!" She looked angry again, more than after the movie. "Those are women you don't even know. They're just abstractions. I'm here! I'm real! Isn't that a million times better?"

Her getting so angry made me nervous. "Also, we don't know each other that well," I said.

Audrey sat up. She reached for a pack of cigarettes near her bed. "Okay, tell me what you want to know."

"It's not any particular thing," I stammered. "It's just—"

She raised her hand like she was giving a speech. "My favorite foods: pomegranates and veal kidneys. My least favorite foods: chocolate pudding with lumps and creamed spinach. Things I don't like to do: go on roller coasters, get my period, watch my mom get depressed when her boyfriend doesn't treat her right.

Things I like: guys with blond, curly hair, real sincerity not just bullshit sincerity, white bulldogs, going to bed at ten on New Year's Eve. What was good about my childhood: learning to play the recorder, scaring my best friend, Marsha, with ghost stories, washing my hair in the rain with Aunt Sally. What was bad about my childhood: Dad's leaving, our moving around too much, getting scarlet fever and missing eight months of school so I was a year older than everybody when I went back." She took a deep breath. "Now you go on."

"You shouldn't smoke," I said, as she started chain-lighting another.

"I'm nervous! I'm horny! I'm depressed! . . . Why shouldn't I smoke?"

I licked my lips. "No, I just meant—it's not good for you."

"Okay, so lots of things aren't good for me. *This* isn't good for me. Being rejected. Ending up with some screwed-up teenage kid who won't even fuck me for a favor, who doesn't even like me—"

I reached over for her. "I do like you. I mean it. I like you a lot."

"Will you sleep over? I won't rape you in the middle of the night. I promise. I just want to feel you there." She got up and put on a nightgown. Then she went and got me some pajamas that she said belonged to her mother's boyfriend. I got into them. They fit pretty well.

"I guess I should call home," I said. "Just so my grandmother won't worry." It was just after midnight, but my grandmother has insomnia and usually stays up till two or three watching the Late Late Show.

"What're you going to tell her?"

I told my grandmother I was staying at Rob's. She never checks. She trusts me implicitly.

Audrey looked at me playfully as I hung up. "You're such a sweetie, good to your grandma." After we got into bed, she said, "Spence, I didn't mean to act weird before. I think it's great, your helping all those women get pregnant. I respect that."

"Well, yeah . . ." I felt a little better.

"It's just pleasure isn't a bad thing. People go around thinking it's easy. It isn't. It's *harder* than being miserable. I can be miserable at the drop of a hat, but the number of times I've ever been really happy, I can count on the fingers of one hand."

I slept really well at Audrey's. That surprised me, because usually I don't sleep well at other people's houses. The only ironical thing was I woke up in the middle of the night and I was hard. I didn't know what to do about it. Maybe Audrey wouldn't have minded if I'd woken her up, but I wasn't sure I wanted to. That's the thing. I do like Audrey, but what if she got pregnant? What if she isn't using anything like she said? I don't feel like I know her well enough yet to know if she'd lie about something like that.

When I woke up in the morning, Audrey had already gotten out of bed. I found her in the kitchen, eating scrambled eggs and bacon. She was dressed in shorts and a plaid shirt. "Want some?" she asked.

"Sure." I sat and watched her fix breakfast for me. She was a good cook. She did the bacon just right, just brown enough, patting the grease off with some paper towels. Bacon and eggs sound simple to make, but so many people, including my grandmother, wreck them somehow.

"You'd really make someone a good wife," I said appreciatively while I was eating.

"On the basis of bacon and eggs?" She laughed.

"Well, that's important, knowing how to cook and all. Everybody has to eat."

She was smiling at me in a teasing way. "Do you cook, Spence?"

"A couple of things—chili, hamburgers, stuff like that."

"You better add to your repertoire, or how can you be a good husband?"

I figured that was a joke. I spread some jam on the toast she'd fixed.

"My husband's father was a chef in a vegetarian restaurant, so he'd learned a lot. And vegetables are good for you," Audrey said. "Low cholesterol. Mike was a real sweetie that way. I'd come home really zonked from my job, and he'd have everything all ready to go. He said cooking relaxed him."

"Maybe that's why your marriage broke up," I suggested.

"I don't get it," Audrey said.

I finished the last slice of bacon. "Well, that's not the way it's supposed to be, exactly—the husband cooking and the wife working."

Audrey started tickling me. "Come on, give me some more of your theories. Should we have a child a year, too?"

I wriggled around. Being tickled gets me excited. "Stop it," I said. "Or I'll get you back."

She backed away, laughing. "Oh, no, that's not fair. Not after I fixed you a great breakfast like that."

I chased her upstairs and pounced on her. I tickled

her all over, until she said, "Spence, really, don't. That's enough." She looked really pretty, all flushed and out of breath. Then she reached down and touched me. Without meaning to or even thinking about it I'd gotten hard. "So, why don't we—" she began.

I pulled back. "Audrey, listen, I just can't, okay?"

"I want to make you happy," she said. "I want to give you pleasure."

"You did," I said. "You do. I really like being with you. I'm not kidding. But I feel like I have to take this job seriously, or what's the point?"

Audrey sighed. "Say, just hypothetically, you quit. Don't they have dozens of other guys whose sperm is just as good?"

"Maybe not," I said, starting to get my breath back. "There're a lot of factors. Some guys come from homes with relatives who were crazy or who had criminal tendencies, all of that. It's not as easy to find people as you think."

Audrey's expression softened. She ran her finger up my back. "But why do it at all, if it just wrecks your social life?"

"It's just for the summer," I said. I lay down beside her. "And anyway, that's like, my philosophy of life, helping other people. That's why I want to be a doctor. Because if you just sit around *thinking* things, *thinking* about doing good, what good does that do? You have to really do it, and you have to make some kind of sacrifice, something that in some way is painful."

"Life isn't painful enough?" Audrey said wryly.

"That doesn't count," I said. "If *you* suffer, but you don't help anyone."

She sat up and kissed me. "You're such a strange

person, Spence, such a sweetie in so many ways, and yet—"

I cleared my throat. "I mean, if you don't want to see me because of this, I'd understand." I said. "Because, maybe you need someone—"

"No." She looked pensive. "Maybe this *is* what I need. Sex just messes everything up in your head. You do it with someone and pretty soon that's all the relationship is, jumping into bed every second. We can really get to know each other. You'll be like my brother. I never had a brother."

I sure have enough sisters, but I was glad she understood.

Probably looking back on this, I'll really regret not taking advantage of what Audrey is offering. But it doesn't seem right, making it with her and then going off to college, where I'll probably meet some other girl. My sisters are always telling me how vulnerable girls are, whether they're virgins or not. And here Audrey already had a marriage that didn't work out. If I did it with her just for the summer, she might start getting a really low opinion of men. I wouldn't want that on my record.

I promised Rob I'd go with him to Wayne State to help him find a room. They'd written him saying the dorms were full and kids were going to have to find rented rooms off campus. Then, once they know some other kids, they can get together and maybe share an apartment. Linc called up and asked Rob if he could go with us.

"And Taffy, too?" I said. I had thought of it as just me and Rob, the way it was in high school when we'd do things together.

"No, just him. She'll stay back with the baby."

"Why does he want to come?" I said. Since Linc's decided not to go to college, at least for now, you'd think it might just make him feel bad.

"He says it'll be like old times," Rob said. "I don't mind if he comes. Do you?"

"Uh-uh." I threw the rest of my stuff in a duffel bag and we drove by Linc's parents' house. He was out waiting for us. As we drove up, Taffy popped out of the house, carrying the baby. "He has a tooth," she called out.

"Good work," I said. She scampered down the steps and held the baby right in front of the window. She pried open his mouth to show me the tooth. It was about halfway through.

"He's been driving us crazy," Linc said. "Screaming all night."

"You should be proud," Taffy said.

Linc climbed in the back seat and threw his bag on top of mine. "So, see you, hon," he said, rubbing the baby on the head.

"When will you be back?" Taffy asked anxiously.

"Probably about—" Rob began, but Linc said, "Don't wait up. We might even stay over. It depends."

"On what?" She looked at the three of us.

"We have to find this guy a place to stay," Linc said. "It might take a while."

Taffy marched back up the steps, looking grim. There was a moment of silence. "Okay, let's move," Linc said. As we turned around the corner, he sighed and leaned back. "Goodbye, house; goodbye, baby; goodbye, wife . . . hello, freedom."

"Hey, Linc," Rob said, "we're just going up to find me a room, that's all."

"We'll see," Linc said expansively. He pulled a beer can out of his bag. "What happens, happens. Remember what Jones used to say, 'Life Is a Happening.'" He handed the beer can up front to me. I took a few swallows and offered it to Rob.

"Not while I'm driving," he said. He looked a little grim, too. "I think you ought to treat Taffy better."

Linc laughed. "Who me? Or him?"

"You, you jerk. You're married to her."

"So, where's the law that says I have to treat her well all the time? Does she treat *me* well all the time? Look, give me a break, okay? You're sitting there free, happy, ready to go off to college. I don't want any fucking lectures."

"Taffy's a nice girl," I put in lamely.

"Sure, she's nice," Linc said. "Hey, did I say she wasn't nice? Did anyone hear me say that? You guys think she's so nice—take her. You can have her, and the baby as a free bonus. What d'you say? How about it?"

"Linc, pipe down," I said. I bet he had a couple of beers before he left home.

"I'm making a once in a lifetime offer," he said. "Wife, baby . . . absolutely free of charge, no tax even."

"I feel like you're breaking her heart," Rob said. He can talk that way sometimes. Maybe it's because he writes poetry in his spare time.

Linc took up my guitar, which I'd brought along. "You're breaking her heart," he crooned in his terrible voice. The guy is unable to carry any kind of tune. "And she's a nice girl . . . no, wait, girl doesn't rhyme with heart does it? What rhymes with heart? Mart? Fart?"

"If you didn't want to marry her," Rob said, "you shouldn't have gotten her pregnant."

"Oh, yeah," Linc said. "Right. That was bad, wasn't it? We did a real bad thing. Unlike you and Edina and Spence and Emmy Lou who just sat around nights, reciting poetry. We turned the lights off. We played doctor. We were *baaad*."

"I never did it with Emmy Lou," I said, just to set the record straight.

"And I never did it with Edina," Rob said. That surprised me. I was sure he had.

"Oh, boy," Linc said, with disgust. "So you're a fine pair to give me advice. Do it, okay? Do it with some girl who swears on a stack of bibles she's on the Pill, and then comes to you in tears and says maybe she just forgot to take one or maybe it was two or even three, or maybe it was really that she was never on the Pill at all. Maybe she was just pretending because she was kind of hoping deep deep down she might get knocked up and some poor sucker just might be addle-brained enough to marry her."

"Taffy wouldn't do that," Rob said.

"I guess you know her real well," Linc said. "How about you, Spence? Let's take a poll. Would Taffy do a thing like that quote unquote? What do you say, Spence? Let's hear it for the heartlands of America."

"I think she might've actually forgotten."

He laughed. "Yeah, well I'll tell you one thing. You are safe as Moses with that chick you brought bowling with us. *She's* not going to forget, I can tell you that."

"Who's that?" Rob asked.

"Her name's Audrey Rummel," I said. "I met her at a travel agency."

"She cannot bowl to save herself," Linc said, "but she has an amazing ass. World-class. Tell her I said so."

"Are you, like, dating her?" Rob said, turning to me.

"Yeah, we've been out a couple of times," I said. I felt uncomfortable talking about Audrey with them. It was different talking about girls we all knew in high school. "But basically we're just friends."

"Friends!" Linc gave a howl of anguish. "Christ, with an ass like that! And she's divorced? . . . What are you, crazy?"

"I don't feel like talking about it," I said.

"Yeah, Linc, shut up, will you?" Rob said. "You're making him nervous. Quiet down. You're making me nervous, too. I'm trying to drive."

Linc was silent a few minutes. "She wants to be a pilot or something?" he said, passing the beer to me again.

"Linc, lay off the beer, will you?" Rob said. "I don't want you puking all over the back seat before we even get there."

Linc rolled open his window and threw the beer can out. "Happy?" he said.

"No," Rob shouted. "You're littering the fucking landscape. Act human!"

"Who's she divorced from?" Linc asked me. "Anyone from around here?"

"No, some older guy," I said. "I guess they're on good terms. He gave her a Honda as a present when they split."

Linc whistled. "Wow . . . why don't I meet girls like that? A Honda!"

"You're not going to meet anyone," Rob said. "You're married."

"You mean it's a life term?" Linc began to gasp in horror. "Please, judge, I didn't mean to do it. It was temporary insanity. Can't I, like, maybe be paroled when I'm thirty? I won't do it again, I promise. I got carried away."

"Put a pillow over his head, will you?" Rob said.

I turned around and put my hand over Linc's mouth. He struggled and then said, "Okay, okay, I can take a hint. Wake me up when we get there. I didn't sleep last night."

Five minutes later he was snoring like a fiend.

"How does Taffy take it?" Rob said. He sighed. "Boy, I guess we *are* lucky. The thing is, Edina just wouldn't do it with me. It wasn't that I had such fantastic willpower. She said she'd only do it if I gave her an engagement ring first."

"Me too," I said. "With Emmy."

"But, like you said, college girls are different," Rob said. "They have career goals. For them sex is just—they want experience, like us. They don't want to be tied down."

I kept thinking of Audrey and wondering if I was crazy. She was so beautiful and nice and understanding. But I really did make this goal for myself, like a test, that I would get through this summer without messing around. It's not like it's for life. But I know, if I can do it, I'll never regret it. It'll be something I'll always be proud of.

When we reached the campus, Rob got out his map and we started driving up and down the side streets where the letter said there were boardinghouses with rooms to rent. A lot of them were taken already, even though it was still just July. But finally, after looking at about ten, Rob came out looking happy. "Great," he said. "It's a little small, but the price is good."

Linc was still sleeping in the back. I thought we might have to set off a small nuclear weapon to wake him up. I helped Rob in with some of his stuff. The landlady watched us a little critically, but then said she could move in a desk and a lamp if he needed one. By then it was getting toward evening. "We could have dinner here," Rob said, "and then head on home."

"Sure," I said.

As we were looking through the pamphlet the college sent out for a good cheap place to eat, Linc woke up. "Where am I?" he said.

"I got a room," Rob said.

"Why didn't you wake me up?"

"You looked like you needed the rest."

Together the three of us found an Italian place that they said was cheap but had the best pizza in town. Actually, I'm not that crazy about pizza, but I like Italian food in general, especially weird things, like calamari in oil and garlic or shrimp marinara.

Linc and Rob decided to share a pizza. "Maybe you better sit over there," Linc said, as the waiter set down my calamari.

"What's wrong?" I said. "It's great."

"You and Taffy would make a perfect pair," he said. "She loves weird foods, too."

A girl at a booth right behind us turned around. "You mean me?" she said. She was fairly cute-looking, with a big mop of blond frizzy hair. "I'm Taffy."

"No, he meant his—" Rob began, but Linc kicked him before the word "wife" had a chance to get out.

"Do *you* have weird tastes?" Linc asked, smiling at her.

"Only in men." She smiled back. She was with some other girls. "You guys from the college?"

I pointed to Rob. "He's starting school in September."

"We're sophomores," she said. She turned back to

her friends and then turned back. "We could show you around, if you'd like."

"Sure," Linc said. "We're game. Show us the town."

"Are *you* going here, too?" the other Taffy said in surprise. "I thought it was him."

"No, he's—" Rob started, but Linc kicked him again so the word "married" got lost in the shuffle.

The booth we were in sat only four people. It was the same with the booth the three girls were in. So, while we were eating, we just talked back and forth a little. Once one of the girls, not Taffy but one of her friends, got up to play something on the jukebox. She was tall and skinny and had on one of those long ruffled skirts and cavalry boots. Her hair was in a black braid down her back. Seeing me looking at her, she said, "It's Duran Duran. Do you like them? They're my favorite group."

The song she was playing was one Roxanne likes, too. "Yeah, they're pretty good," I said.

"Only pretty good?" She laughed and sat down again with her friends. "You must have discriminating tastes."

"So do we," Linc called out. "We have discriminating tastes, too!"

The waiter had brought our check. We divided up the amount and paid. Then Rob lowered his voice, "I guess we better, you know, explain the situation."

"What situation?" Linc said.

"Well, we can't just go picking up some girls with Taffy waiting for you back home."

Linc rolled his eyes. "Who's Taffy?" he said.

At that the other Taffy turned around. "Me!" she

said. "You can remember because I have taffy-colored hair. That's how I got the nickname."

Linc leapt to his feet. "I love girls with taffy-colored hair," he said, putting his hand on her head.

Rob looked at me and shrugged. "I guess it's not our problem," he said.

But I knew what he meant. If Linc had been married to just anyone, I wouldn't have cared. But I like Taffy, and I felt bad thinking of her sitting around at home with that funny-looking baby with the tooth coming in. Meanwhile, Linc and the other Taffy were walking out the door, and the other two girls were standing around, waiting for us to make some move.

"You said you wanted us to show you around," one of the girls said, not the one with the braid.

Rob got up slowly. "Okay, sure," he said reluctantly. He walked off with her. She was short and round and was wearing a big felt hat.

The girl with the braid told me her name was Beverly. "Doesn't your friend like girls?" she said. "The tall one?"

"Yeah, he likes them," I said slowly. I half wanted to protect Linc, not to tell he was married. "It's something else."

She walked along beside me, her boots clicking on the pavement. "My brother's like that. He likes women, but he also likes men. He says everyone is a little like that, but we don't all act on it."

I felt embarrassed. "It's not that," I said. "It's something completely different."

Ahead of us, Linc and the other Taffy were walking arm in arm. "I guess your short friend doesn't have that problem," Beverly said. "Short guys are always ready to go. I don't know why that is."

"Is her name really Taffy?" I said. That seemed like a weird kind of coincidence.

"Yeah, why shouldn't it be?"

I shrugged. I felt totally out of it. I'd drunk two glasses of red wine at dinner, and wine can do that to me. I don't get drunk, exactly, but I feel far away, like whatever is happening already happened and I'm just remembering it the next day. I hate that feeling.

It turned out the girls had an old beat-up station wagon, and their intention was to drive us around the campus, pointing out the sights. The short girl, whose name was Maureen, sat in front with Rob, I sat in back with Beverly, and Linc and the other Taffy were stretched out in the way back part, where you usually put luggage. I didn't even feel like turning around and seeing what was going on back there.

"This is basically what they call Collegetown." Maureen said. "This whole row of stores. Most of us never go down into the town proper because it's such a long trip."

"Where are you going to school?" Beverly asked me. I was relieved that she sat a few inches away from me and didn't act that clinging.

I told her.

"I've heard that's a good school," she said. "I only came here because of the medical school. I heard it's easier to get in if you were an undergraduate here."

I said I wanted to be a doctor, too. It wasn't a relaxed conversation, though—for me, anyway. All the time we were talking I kept hearing these muffled squeaks and murmurs from the back of the car. It could have been the wine, but I started feeling really tense. I opened the car window.

There was a squeal from the back. "Hey, it's cold," the other Taffy said.

"It's ninety degrees out," Maureen said. "How can you be cold?" She turned around. It was a red light. "Hey, Taff, behave yourself, okay?"

"I am," Taffy said, and giggled.

"She gets an A for good behavior," Linc said.

After they'd driven us around, the girls asked if we felt like going up to their place and smoking some pot. It was midnight. Rob said, "I don't know, I think maybe we ought to head home. It's getting kind of late."

"Stay over," Maureen said cheerfully. "We've got extra space. We rented this whole house. Wait till you see it."

Rob looked at me. I'd promised I'd drive back, since he'd driven there, but to tell the truth, I felt crummy. I just wanted to go to sleep. "We can get up early," I said, "make an early start."

I knew Rob didn't know if that meant I was interested in Beverly or what. I could tell he wasn't all that interested in Maureen. Ironically, the only two who really seemed to be hitting it off were Linc and the other Taffy. On the way up the steps, Rob muttered under his breath to me, "I don't know if we should be doing this."

"I just feel too zonked to drive," I admitted.

"Me, too."

The house was a big old ramshackle house, like the kind Willa and her husband live in. But unlike Willa's, it wasn't fixed up much. Just a few old rag rugs and some kind of broken-down furniture.

"Want one of the guest bedrooms?" Beverly asked.

81

She put her hand on my shoulder. "You don't look too good."

"I'll be okay," I said, though I felt like I was about to go sliding to the floor. Beverly was really nice about the whole thing. I can't even remember all of it, but she got me to this room with a bed in it, and I must have passed out pretty much when I hit the pillow.

When I woke up, it was early, between five and six, just starting to get light. I felt okay, just kind of stiff, and my mouth was furry. I washed up in the bathroom, and that helped a whole lot. Then I went downstairs. Rob was already up, reading, in the living room. "I couldn't sleep," he said. "Can you drive? Because I feel like hell."

"Yeah, I can drive," I said. I looked around. The house was so silent, it was spooky. "Where is everyone?"

"Beverly's out jogging." He sighed and threw the paper on the floor. "I guess everyone else is still alseep."

We were silent a minute. "So, what do you want to do? Wake him up or what?" I asked, stretching.

Rob scratched his head. "Let's go out and get some breakfast. Maybe by the time we come back, he'll be up."

We found a diner in Collegetown that made fresh coffee cake. The smell filled the whole place. Over coffee Rob said, "You know, I knew this would happen. I had this premonition while we were setting out. I know you don't believe in all that, but I did."

The reason I don't believe in it is that most premonitions seem to me like someone looking out the window, seeing it's cloudy, and having a "premonition" it may rain. "We're not our brother's keeper," I said, biting into the coffee cake.

"Yeah," Rob said gloomily. "Right . . . only maybe we are. I mean, when does that apply and when doesn't it?"

"I don't know." The coffee was good, hot and strong, the way I like it.

"Say, just for instance, Taffy was my sister or your sister? Would we have stayed?"

"Probably not."

Rob's face looked all red and wrinkled, the way my grandparents' dog looks when he's been away a few days and finally turns up. "I hate Linc," he said. "He's not my friend anymore. He's just a goddamn jerk."

"He can be a nice guy," I said. The coffee cake was so good I went up to get some more.

"He's got the morals of a snake," Rob said, when I came back. "He doesn't even deserve Taffy. And now what're we supposed to do? Lie to her?"

I hadn't thought of that. "I think we better."

"I hate that," Rob said fiercely. "*He* did something wrong so *we* have to lie! He did that to me in junior year, when he kept cutting football practice and I had to make up excuses for him. I feel like maybe I'm some kind of patsy. I just let him use me. It's my own damn fault."

I knew what Rob meant, only somehow, maybe just out of feeling physically good, having slept well and having had a good breakfast, I didn't feel it the way he did. Also, Linc was always more Rob's friend than mine. He was my friend, too, but we were never all that close.

"What does it show?" Rob asked me intensely. It

seems like ever since we've been friends, Rob wants me to sum everything up for him, to give it some kind of moral. I try my best, but lots of times I'm not sure.

I looked out the window. "Maybe it shows you shouldn't mess around with girls or women or whatever unless you're going to give it your all."

Rob nodded. "You've got to go the distance," he said solemnly. "Remember how Coach Markey always said that? Not in physical terms, but you've got to put your whole soul in every little thing you do."

"Right," I said. I thought about how I feel coming out of RGC, how I know at those times I'm doing something good and I feel this terrific kind of peacefulness. Once, right after RGC, I went into a drugstore for something, and there was this pregnant woman. Obviously I couldn't have made her pregnant, since she was quite far gone, in her seventh or eighth month, easy. And sure, lots of pregnant women just look grumpy or gigantic in a swollen, ugly way. But this woman—I guess she was Lizzie's age—turned and looked at me, and I swear she somehow knew where I'd been and what I'd just been doing. She had this radiant, grateful expression. I practically thought she was going to embrace me, but it wasn't a sexual thing. It was out of pure, altruistic love.

But the trouble is, you have these moments and they don't last. On the way back to the girls' house with Rob, I thought of Audrey and how to her I must seem like just some kind of screwed-up, neurotic jerk, and how, when I try to explain myself to her, it comes out sounding awkward and idiotic and rationalizing. "We're all jerks," I said suddenly. "We all act like jerks with women."

"No, we don't," Rob said, looking hurt. "We do not, *I* don't."

"You said in the car the only reason you didn't make it with Edina was she wouldn't do it unless you gave her a ring."

"Yeah, so? What's so bad about that? She's still intact, for what that's worth. I didn't, like, sully her virtue or anything. What would be bad is if I'd promised her a ring, knowing I wasn't going to give one to her."

He was looking so rotten, I just said, "No, that's true. I see your point."

Luckily, by the time we got back to the house Linc was up, doing some exercises in the living room. Maureen and Beverly were putting around in the kitchen. There was a smell of coffee.

"You guys must've gotten up early," Linc said, bending.

The guy really has muscles. He must still lift weights every day. "We're ready to set out," Rob said tightly.

"Okay," Linc said. "Let me get a bowl of cereal, okay? My stuff's all ready."

Rob sat down in a rocker and reread the paper; I just stood near the window and watched various people jogging by. Finally, Linc gave me a poke. "Ready to hit the road?"

The girls came out to say goodbye. "Don't mind Taffy," Beverly said. "She never gets up before noon on Sunday."

"So give us a ring when you come back in September," Maureen said to Rob.

"Good luck with your studies," Beverly called to me as I drove off.

"Same to you," I called. We drove on in silence.

"Nice girls," Linc remarked from the back seat, where he was stretched out, his feet up against the window.

I could feel Rob tensing up. Suddenly he turned around and said, "So, what do you expect us to tell Taffy? You didn't even call her! You didn't even tell her you'd be back this late."

"Sure I did," Linc said, sounding annoyed. "I told her not to wait up. You heard me, didn't you, Spence? I said we didn't know how long it'd take to find you a room and we might stay over. So we stayed over."

Rob was getting all red and flustered, the way he always does when he's upset. "We ought to just dump you out of the car and let you walk home."

"Relax," Linc said. "I didn't touch her."

"You're full of shit."

"What were you—peeking through the goddamn keyhole? I told you, I didn't touch her. You want to call her up and ask? Go ahead. Let's pull off at the next phone booth, and you call her."

Out of the corner of my eye I saw a phone booth.

"You know I'm not going to do that," Rob muttered.

Linc snorted. "You spend half of high school coming to me, 'What can I do to get Edina to do it? Should I do this? Should I do that? Is it okay to lie?' And now suddenly you're this big moralist!"

"You're married!" Rob shouted.

"Okay, so you've been married so many times you're giving me advice? Tell me about it. I want to hear about all your marriages, all your fucking wives and how you treated them."

Suddenly Rob half dove over the seat, and in one

second the two of them were tumbling around, fighting. By mistake, someone's foot kicked me in the neck. The car swerved to one side, and we ended up in a ditch. I turned around and grabbed both of them. "Hey, you want to get us killed? You're both jerks. I'm going to pitch you *both* out and have you *both* walk home!"

Linc must've given Rob some kind of black eye. He looked even worse than he had before. "I'm the one who loves Taffy," I said. "She was *my* girlfriend. What are you two fighting about?"

I don't know why I said "love." I shouldn't have. "You *love* Taffy?" Linc said.

"I love her like a sister," I amended. "That's what I meant."

Rob climbed back over to the front seat. "Me, too. I love her like a sister, too."

No one said anything for about fifteen minutes. I was basically concentrating on the driving and relieved the fight was over.

"I'm a shit," Linc said. "It's true. Taffy should've married a better guy."

Rob turned around again. "Listen, I'm just asking you this because we're friends. I won't get mad again, I promise. . . . Did you really not lay a hand on the other Taffy?"

Linc sighed. "No, I lied," he said. "We did it three times, and it was terrific. Each time was better than the last."

Rob folded his arms. "Then you are a shit," he said.

Linc was silent.

"It's over," I said. "Let's forget it." I was glad I

was driving. After a while I glanced over and saw that Rob was asleep.

When we got back to town, we dropped Linc off first. Taffy came scampering out, just like she had when we left. "How was it? Did you get a room?" she asked Rob. She seemed so innocent and unknowing, I felt rotten. I know Rob did, too. Then she gasped at the sight of Rob's eyes, which was all swollen and discolored. "What happened to your eye?"

"Oh, it just . . . it's some kind of allergy," Rob said.

Of all the dumb possible lies! An allergy! But Taffy came over and looked at him with concern. "Goodness, it looks like you were in a fight."

"It just happens from time to time," Rob went on. "It goes away."

Linc had gotten out of the car. He shook my hand and reached over to shake Rob's. "No hard feelings, right?" he said.

"Sure," I said quickly. What else was I going to say with Taffy standing just a few feet behind him?

"We're all human," he amended. Then he turned and walked, his arm around Taffy, into the house.

As we drove off, Rob said, "We're all human? Boy, what shit! . . . I don't think we all *are* human, personally. Or at least some us are more human than others."

I glanced at him. "How's your allergy?"

He looked sheepish. "I'm not a good liar, am I? Mom says that's one of my endearing traits."

I pulled up in front of Rob's house. "Well, anyway, you got a room," I said.

"Yeah, I got a room." He climbed out of the car. As he did I saw his father come loping slowly over to us. He was wearing aviator sunglasses and a bright yellow short-sleeved shirt.

"You were gone all night," he said good-humoredly to Rob. "What happened? Some cute coeds drag you back to their lair?"

"No, nothing like that," Rob said. "But I got a room."

"Good for you. Tell me about it." They walked off together, and I drove the car back to my grandparents' house.

Lizzie, June, and I drove my grandparents to the airport on the evening of their trip. Willa and Carnie couldn't make it, and anyway, if they had, we would've had to take a separate car. This way we all managed to squeeze in. My grandmother drove. She distrusts anyone who goes over forty miles an hour, which includes just about everybody who's allowed on the road. Even when I've sworn to her I won't "speed," as she puts it, I find myself automatically going fifty or sixty. At forty you see half the cars on the road passing you, or else the drivers looking at you like you're crazy. But everyone in the family has come to accept it. When my grandmother is driving, you just add on an extra hour to what it would normally take.

It was nine in the evening. The heat had let up just a little, and there was a cool breeze. I helped them with their luggage. June was holding my grandfather's arm.

He claims he doesn't need help walking, but he's fallen a few times.

First we checked their luggage through. "You look like you must be honeymooners," the man behind the ticket counter said, winking at me.

My grandfather narrowed his eyes. "We're living in sin," he snarled. "My third wife won't divorce me."

"Don't tell me," the man said, impervious to my grandfather's sarcastic tone. "When they've got you by the balls, they just won't let go, will they?"

As we walked off, my grandfather started to mutter. "What kind of people are they hiring these days? Scum? Idiots? Honeymooners indeed!"

"Dear, it was a compliment," my grandmother said, taking his arm. "He thought we looked young."

We waited for the boarding announcement. "I feel exhausted already," my grandfather said, collapsing in a chair.

"Once you're there, you can relax," June said. "You'll have nothing to do *but* relax."

"Why aren't you young people going?" he said. "*You'd* really enjoy it. Come on, how about it?" He looked at me and then at June and Lizzie. "Take our tickets."

Boy, was I tempted, but Lizzie said, "Grandpa, you deserve some fun and pleasure out of life."

"No, I don't," he said. "I'm just a selfish old beast. I don't deserve anything."

"You're an old darling," June crooned. "And you're going to have the time of your life."

My grandmother was sitting tensely on the edge of her seat, waiting for the announcement. She's very nervous about arrivals and departures. She'd been up since five in the morning, checking "last-minute details." The second the voice on the loudspeaker said, "We are now ready to board passengers on Flight 101," my grandmother was out of her seat like a shot. She yanked my grandfather to his feet.

"Take it easy, Peg," my grandfather said. "They won't leave without us." We helped them down the walkway to the place where the attendant was taking tickets. Lizzie and June kissed my grandmother and then my grandfather. I just stood to one side, feeling awkward.

"Have a super time!" Lizzie called, as they started off to the plane.

"Oh, I hope they will," June sighed, as soon as they were out of earshot. "Do you think they will?"

Since it was too late to do anything about it and it was her money, I said, "Sure, they'll have fun," though I privately doubted it.

"It was a sweet thought, Junie," Lizzie said. "I wish I'd thought of it myself." She turned to both of us. "Let's have a drink before we head back, okay?"

We went to the cocktail lounge. Lizzie ordered a margarita like she always does, June asked for a gin and tonic, and I had a beer.

"I used to think of gin and tonics when I was in the convent," June said in her soft, thoughtful voice. "It was terrible. Here I gave up sex and didn't even miss it, but cigarettes and gin and tonics were all I thought of all the time."

"I truly don't know how you did it," Lizzie exclaimed. "Six years! Come on, you really didn't think of sex in six whole years?"

"Oh, I thought of it," June said, lighting up a cigarette, "but not in that painful, yearning way. Maybe I'm undersexed or something."

Lizzie ran her tongue around the edge of the glass to lick the salt. "I'd last a week, tops, then I'd take a flying leap on top of some poor sexy old priest."

"Listen, they had a lineup, some of them," June said. "You wouldn't have been the only one."

Watching June smoke, I thought of Audrey. "My girlfriend smokes a lot," I said. "I wish she'd stop."

"Which girlfriend is that?" Lizzie asked, reaching for the bowl of peanuts. "A new one?"

I told them a little about Audrey. I know my sisters think I'm more sexually experienced than I am.

"She sounds great," June said. "That's what you need, Spence, someone more sophisticated and relaxed. That Emmy Lou wasn't worthy of you."

"Remember her nails?" Lizzie laughed. Emmy Lou had long pink nails that she painted every night. Once when she broke one, I thought she was going to have a heart attack."

"You know who *I* always thought was sweet," June said. "That little Taffy, the one with the braids who sent you ten valentines that one year."

I'd forgotten that. It was in seventh grade. At first when I started opening them, I thought they were all from different girls and I was amazed at how popular I was; but then I saw a little T at the bottom of each card. "She's married now," I said, "with a baby."

"Lord," Lizzie said, "How can that be? That little girl?"

"Babies having babies," June said. "It's a tragedy."

"They don't know what they're doing!" Lizzie said. "Their idea of sex education is closing their eyes and praying."

"It's sexism, pure and simple," June went on.

"Here boys can walk in *any* drugstore and buy contraceptives, and girls have to go on hands and knees to a doctor, praying he won't give them a lecture on what evil monsters they are!"

"How about the sponge?" Lizzie had finished her drink and ordered another.

"Is it tested, though?" June said. "And how would *you* like to stick in a sponge every time?" Suddenly she glanced at me. "Spence, don't take any of this personally."

I'd had enough beer so I was feeling pretty mellow. Anyway, I've heard my sisters talk a lot about this, especially Lizzie and June. Willa is much more conservative, and so's Carnie. "I don't," I said. "All men are different."

Lizzie was starting her second margarita. "Actually, that's not true," she said. "All men are pretty much the same . . . but some are a little different."

"All women are pretty much the same," I countered.

"No," Lizzie insisted, leaning toward me. She looked pretty in the dim light. "There, you're wrong. Women are all totally different. Maybe it's having wombs. Do you think that's it?" she asked June.

"Do I think what's what?" June asked. She had only drunk a third of her gin and tonic. She's not really much of a drinker.

"Men are just—" Lizzie gestured, trying to figure out what she wanted to say. She looked all excited and hyper, the way she does when she's a little high. "It's the impervious thing. I think that's it. Women have wombs so they have some built-in capacity to relate, and men are just there, watching. It's the capacity to reproduce. You—"

"*I* have the capacity to reproduce," I interrupted. I had the feeling we were talking too loud. "Look at me. I've probably reproduced more than either of you will ever do."

"I don't know if that counts," Lizzie said.

"Ten million sperm in every ejaculation," I boasted. I was a little high myself, but in a good way. It may also have been the thought that my grandparents would be gone for two whole blessed weeks.

When we finished our drinks, I drove them both home and then went back to our house. In some ways I was looking forward to living alone for two weeks, not having to get up at any special time or have meals at any special time, not having to listen to my grandfather's lectures or my grandmother's anxious questions. But there's also something a little spooky about being in such a big house by yourself. It has three floors and six bedrooms. After my sisters grew up, my grandparents thought of moving and even looked at some houses but my grandmother always said she loved the house, even if it was a lot of work. I'm not afraid of burglars, exactly—we live in a pretty safe neighborhood. I just got a strange feeling coming back alone.

I remembered how Audrey had gone around flipping on all the lights because her mother wasn't going to be there. I could have Audrey over! She could stay all weekend. But maybe that was a bad idea. Instead, maybe it would be good to set myself a really strict schedule: up early, jogging, checking in with Merc to see if he had any jobs for me, going twice a week to RGC. Maybe I shouldn't see Audrey at all in these two weeks. I got into bed, still not sure what I ought to do. I knew Rob and Linc would think I was a fool not to take advantage of this opportunity. Then the phone rang.

It was Audrey. "Hi, sweetie," she said. "Were you alseep?"

"Not yet." I hadn't seen her since the trip I'd taken with Linc and Rob. "Are you okay?"

"Yeah . . . I just wanted to say I hope I didn't come on too strong the other night."

"No, I understand," I said. "Women have needs, too."

"You're a thoughtful guy with a wonderful body, and someday you'll make some lucky girl delirious with happiness," Audrey said.

"Well—I don't know," I began, embarrassed.

"I wanted it to be me," she said. "I guess I wanted to, like, initiate you, make you happy, too. . . . But I've been thinking, and I think this'll be a real test of *my* character too. I've always used sex with guys as a way of establishing a relationship before it really existed. But this way we'll get to know each other."

"Right," I said. I was glad she was looking at it that way. We made plans to see each other over the weekend, and I went back to sleep.

# 10

"Here it is." I set my sample down in the glass jar on the secretary's desk. It was a new secretary. Or at least she'd never been there the other days.

She lifted the jar up by her fingertips. "Are you Number Twenty-two?" she said.

"Yeah." They give you a number, I guess to keep your sperm separate from all the rest.

She looked at me suspiciously. "You don't look like you have American Indian blood," she said.

"I don't."

She began rummaging through a file of papers. "Let's see . . . Number—which number did you say you were?"

"Twenty-two."

"Oh, well, no wonder. They've sent up the wrong file." She shook her head. "Would you mind waiting here while I check on this? It's my first week on the job, and I don't want to make any mistakes."

She scurried off into some other part of the clinic. I

stood there for a while, and then I glanced down and saw the edge of one of the forms sticking out from the folder. I pulled it out. It was me.

## DONOR NO. 22

Summary: Good intellectual and musical ability, outgoing personality, and very good looks.

Ancestry: Northwest European. Born 1960s.

Eye color: Blue.

Skin color: Light.

Hair: Blond (very curly).

Height: 1.8m. (6'0").

Weight: 77kg. (170 lb.).

General appearance: Normal with high cheekbones; very handsome.

Personality: Easygoing, good-natured. Showed early musical ability in trumpet, soloist at church. Athletic achievements in track and swimming.

Achievements: He has an all-A record at school. Won Honor Society Essay on Ethics. Has a Merit Scholarship at a good university.

I.Q.: Not known; scored 700 in math on SAT.

Music: He has an unusual singing voice and was in the school orchestra for six years.

Athletics: No prizes, but was on track team. Swam competitively in first two years of high school. Two relatives were swimming champions.

Manual dexterity: Excellent.

General health: Excellent.

Defects: Impacted wisdom teeth. Two grandparents developed cataracts in their seventies.

Blood type: O +. Pressure: 122/80

Comment: The estimated recurrence rate is 40 percent for impacted wisdom teeth and 22 percent for cataracts developing after age 70.

It was a really weird feeling seeing all this information about myself written up that way, so cut and dried. I'd imagined it was different. I thought they showed the women my photo, at least. In a lot of ways I think this chart is misleading. It leaves off a lot of my best qualities, but also some of my bad ones. Or maybe what I mean to say is it seems like this chart could apply to lots of people. But what makes me special and different isn't on it. Who cares, for instance, if my grandparents had cataracts? Or about my dumb wisdom teeth! It's like they're describing an animal, almost—nothing about your spiritual qualities or your soul.

Even some of the good things are not the way they say. I do have a good singing voice. They say I inherited it from my mother, who used to sing in the church choir and thought of being an opera singer once. But the main reason I joined the choir was it gave my grandmother such a kick. And it was the same with the trumpet. Lizzie led the school orchestra, and she practically forced me to take an instrument. If I didn't practice, she went at me so much that after awhile I did practice and got pretty good. But, let's face it, I'll probably never sing *or* play the trumpet again. Still, I guess what they're figuring is maybe some guy with my genes will really enjoy those things and at least he'll be good at them. It would be sad if someone wanted to play the trumpet a whole lot and he didn't have the genes for it. Or he wanted to sing and, like Rob, he was just totally tone deaf.

I'd put the form describing me back in the folder and was just sitting there, thinking about it, when the new secretary came bustling back in. "They can't find it," she said, almost tearfully. "Which number did you say you were?"

"Twenty-two," I said.

She opened up the folder and looked down. "Well, goodness. Here it is, right under my nose. Isn't that awful? I'm just so nervous, I'm not even *seeing* straight. . . . No, it's that they have the numbers mixed up." She held up the file to show me. "Number Twenty-three is filed *ahead* of Twenty-two." She picked up the sample and stuck a Number 22 label on it. "Thank you so much, Mr. Searles. I'm extremely sorry for the mix up."

"That's okay," I said.

"You're performing a valuable service for your community," she said. "You should be very proud."

"Thank you."

I know it's not allowed, but I wish they'd tell you how many women picked your file. It would be interesting to be there while they were going through, deciding. But, like I say, what if someone picked me just because of my singing voice, which isn't even important, or my curly hair or blue eyes? And what if someone who would really pick me if they met me didn't pick me because I didn't sound like that interesting a person? Here I sat and talked to that doctor for over an hour! We talked about dozens of things, and all they put down was that I was easygoing and relaxed. I'm not. I don't think I'm tense and crazy, but I'm actually a lot less easygoing than I seem. People think I never worry about things, but I do.

For some reason I kept thinking about this all day. I imagined some little boy, maybe six or seven, saying to his mother, "Do I *have* to practice the trumpet?" and she'd say, "Your father was a wonderful musician. Don't you want to be like him?"

They ought to just let kids be what they want and forget about their relatives and all that inherited stuff. But one thing is true—I look almost exactly like my father did at my age. There's a photo of him from high school—he was captain of the basketball team—and we could almost be twins. He even squinted in photos like I do. God, sometimes I wish so much I could know him and talk to him! My sisters and my grandmother are nice people, but they look at everything from a woman's point of view. I wish I could talk to him about Audrey. I wonder if he had any serious girlfriends before he met my mother. They knew each other in high school, but they didn't get married till they were in college.

That evening I went to pick Audrey up. Her mother was there, about to go out. She doesn't look at all like Audrey. She's tall and thin and has long hair pulled straight back. The only thing that's the same is that she's a chain smoker and she has pretty hazel eyes. "I've wanted to meet you, Spencer," she said. "Audrey's told me a lot about you."

I wondered exactly what Audrey had told her. It

mustn't have been that bad, because she looked friendly.

"Are your grandparents having a nice vacation?" Mrs. Rummel asked. "I've heard St. Maarten is lovely."

"I haven't heard from them yet," I said.

"They'll probably have the time of their lives," she went on. "Except the heat can get pretty fierce in July. Can't it, Audrey?"

"Yeah, only the hotels are all air-conditioned," Audrey said.

"It was certainly a thoughtful gesture on your sister's part," Mrs. Rummel said.

"He has four of them," Audrey put in. "Just like you, Mom."

"Oh, goodness. I thought no one was having families that size anymore nowadays," she said. "It practically drove our mother into the ground, let me tell you."

A few minutes later there was a honk or two outside. Mrs. Rummel jumped up, got her bag, and waved goodbye to us. "Nice to have met you, Spencer," she said. "Come again."

Audrey went over and peeked through the curtain. "What's *wrong* with that guy? He can't even get out of the car and help her with her bag?" She gave a snort. "He knows I don't like him, so he doesn't even come in if he thinks I'll be here. . . . Did you like her?"

"Yeah, she seemed nice."

"She's almost forty, and as far as men go, she's like an eleven-year-old. She lets this guy treat her however he feels like. It just gets me so *so* mad!"

"That he's married?" I said. Lizzie once saw some

104

man who was married, and when my grandparents found out, they almost skinned her alive.

"That, that he lies, takes money from her. He's not going to leave his wife any more than I'm going to fly to the moon, but she just believes whatever he says. I hate it when men do that!" She looked at me angrily.

"I don't," I said quickly. "I don't lie."

Audrey came over and ran her fingers through my hair. "No, you're a sweetie. . . . What do you want to do? Go for a drive?"

"Sure."

We took Audrey's car again, but this time, since there weren't any good movies playing, we just drove around. I took her down to the path near the river where I used to run in high school. "I should have known you then," Audrey said wistfully.

"Why?"

"Because then we could've—you didn't have that job."

I put my arms around Audrey and hugged her tight. "Yeah, that would've been great."

Audrey began kissing me along my neck and collarbone. "I really care about you a lot, Spence."

"I care about you, too." We lay down together in the grass. Pretty soon Audrey's hands were under my shirt, sliding up along my back and shoulders and then down again in that magical way she has. She let me take her blouse off and caress her breasts, not even stopping me when I tried to kiss them or take her nipples in my mouth. Emmy Lou used to think that was disgusting. Plus, she said it hurt and she was afraid it wasn't good for her breasts. I don't know what it was that made us finally do it. Maybe it was being there in the dark, beautiful summer night, the stars, the smell of the grass, Audrey being so quiet and soft, letting my hands go anywhere they wanted. Anyway, when she finally reached down and touched me and I was hard, I let her guide me inside her. After that, I couldn't go back. Well, maybe some can, but I stopped even trying to decide what to do at that point. I just moved inside her slowly, like I was swimming in space. Maybe that's how astronauts feel, free of space and time and everything else that ever bothered them or held them down. It was such a fantastic feeling that when I came, I just about passed out. Or at least my mind seemed to dissolve into a big patch of blackness with a few stars glimmering in it. When I came to, Audrey was lying there, her head on my shoulder.

"Was it okay?" she asked gently.

"Yeah, it was great." Boy, what a hypocrite I was!

I thought of all the promises I'd made to myself about the summer. I hadn't even lasted a month! All that stuff about high ideals, and all it took was one girl and one summer night. I feel like they should have put down on that chart that I'm a weak, malleable person who'd do anything if he's with a sexy girl on a beautiful summer night.

"You're so good," Audrey said. "Most guys rush it at the beginning, but you took your time. You wanted me to enjoy it, too."

I sat up and stared off over the river. You could see the lights of some houses on the other bank. "I feel so stupid."

"Why?" Audrey sounded alarmed.

"What kind of person am I? I promised myself I wouldn't have sex with anyone this summer."

"Well, *we* got carried away," Audrey said gently. "That's okay."

"No, it's not! We just *met* a couple of weeks ago. You don't know anything about me."

"Sure I do, Spence. Anyhow, knowing isn't just facts. I know lots about you. I happen to be a very observant person."

"I don't even know why you like me," I admitted. "Is it just for sex?"

She laughed. "Listen, you want to know how many guys proposition me each day? You want me to make a tape for you? You want to know how many dumb come-on lines I've heard just in the last *week*? If all I was interested in was sex, I could've gotten laid ten *times* today alone!" She was getting dressed quickly, pulling her clothes on.

"I'm sorry, Audrey, really. I didn't mean it the way I said."

"So, how *did* you mean it? Look, Spence, there are nice things about you, but I think you've got an awful lot of growing up to do. I think you had the right idea all along. Just spend your summer jerking off into a little cup and have whatever fantasies you want to have about women you'll never meet. I think that's all you really need or want at this point."

That hurt. "I'm *not* just jerking off into a little cup," I said. "I'm performing a valuable service for my community."

"Okay, service every unhappy housewife for miles around," she shouted. "If that's your idea of a perfect sex life, fine. Welcome to it."

"It has nothing to do with sex," I shouted back.

"You're just a baby," she yelled. "A mixed-up baby who happens to have beautiful blue eyes and a great build. Guys who look like you are *always* dopes. It's like Mom says: Fancy wrapping, but nothing inside."

That really got to me. Talk about going for blood! But I was dressed now, so I scrambled up the hill. Then I realized we'd taken her car and we were way out in the middle of nowhere.

"Get in," Audrey said in peremptory voice. "I'll drive you home."

"Forget it," I said.

Her face softened. "Spence, come *on*. We both got overheated. I don't want you dragging along the highway at night. It's dangerous."

"I know the way home from here." I tried to give her a cool stare. "Maybe you can pick someone up on the way home."

She jumped into the car and zoomed off.

Okay, I know that last remark was unkind, but why did she say those things?

*She* should talk about looks! If *she* didn't have a great body and beautiful eyes, none of this would've happened.

It's three miles back to our house. I was glad to be able to work off some of what I felt. I was pretty tired, though, what with having jogged earlier in the day and what had happened down by the river. Also, though I tried to think of anything but what she had said, certain remarks of Audrey kept echoing in my mind. "Fancy wrapping . . . jerking off in a little cup . . ." Fuck her. She's two years older than me anyway. She's divorced, bitter about men. There are a million girls in the world.

Back at the house, I stopped. I was out of breath and exhausted, with a kind of bitter, angry feeling still coursing around somewhere deep inside me, like some

108

aftertaste you can't get rid of. It was still a beautiful night. I went around to the back of our house. We have a big backyard, almost two acres, with a set of garden equipment toward the back, a two-way swing set, a table, some chairs. As I got closer, I saw that the swing was moving back and forth. Someone was in it. My heart started pounding. I wondered if anyone had been casing our house and had decided to make a move now that my grandparents were gone. But all of a sudden a familiar voice called out in a whisper, "Spence?"

It was Taffy. I moved closer and saw that she was sitting on the swing. She was wearing a long white dress and over it a windbreaker. "What're you doing here?" I asked.

"Oh . . . just swinging," she said. "You have such a pretty garden."

I felt worried. "Does Linc know you're here?"

Taffy laughed her soft, whispery laugh. She looked pale and wispy in the moonlight. "No, he's sound asleep. He never wakes up."

"Well, what're you here for?"

"I just like being here," Taffy said. She motioned to the swing. "Do you want to get in?"

I didn't, especially. What I felt like doing was taking a hot shower and going to bed. But I climbed in and sat opposite her. She just had her nightgown on! "Taffy, you ought'd go home," I said nervously. "Do you want me to drive you? It's—it's real late."

"I know," she said. "That's okay. Web always wakes up at one for his late feeding. I always time it. I never stay here till later than twelve-thirty."

"What do you mean never? Have you been here before?"

109

Taffy smiled. "Oh, yeah, I come here a couple of times a week."

"What for?"

"I just feel happy here. Sometimes I look in and see your window, I see you moving around, getting ready for bed. It makes me feel good. . . . Spence, remember that time you had that party when you were twelve?"

I did, because it was the first party I gave where I invited girls. "Yeah?"

"Well, there was this one game, kind of like spin the bottle, where you took the girls off to this swing, only because it was your birthday, you got to pick whoever you wanted. And you picked me! I never knew if it was because my name came first, Armstrong, because for second you picked Bess Benton. . . . Was that it?"

"I don't remember," I said. I leaned forward. "Taffy, seriously, I don't think you ought to be doing this."

"Why not?" Taffy's eyes looked big and milky in the dim light.

"Well, for one, I don't think Linc would like it."

"Oh, he doesn't care," Taffy said. "He wouldn't care if I died. He hates me."

Taffy's usually so light-hearted that those words sounded even worse coming from her than they would have from another person. "He doesn't hate you, Taff." I took her hand. "Really. I *know* he doesn't."

"Yeah, he does." Taffy's voice was gentle and resigned. "And I hate him. And we both hate the baby. That's how it is, Spence. Everybody hates everybody."

I stroked her hand. "No, that's just the way you feel now. It's just a mood."

"Is it?" Taffy's face was so close to mine, I could smell the scent of her skin. Suddenly I felt aroused again. Then I thought of what had happened earlier in the evening and dropped her hand like a hot potato.

"Sure," I said, standing up. I got out of the swing. "You'll feel better in the morning. I get moods like that, too, where everything seems worthless and I know I've done the wrong thing . . ."

"Do you?" Taffy sounded relieved. "You always seem so perfect, like you *never* do the wrong thing."

"I'm *not* perfect," I said, laughing bitterly. "Not by a long shot."

"To me you are," Taffy said. "You're the most perfect person I know."

"You just don't know me that well," I said, hearing that argument with Audrey in the back of my mind.

Taffy climbed out of the swing. It was funny—she was the one who should've been upset, wandering around at night in her nightgown, with Linc not even knowing where she was, but she just seemed dreamy and spaced out, like she was on something. But Taffy doesn't do drugs. I knew it wasn't that. "I guess I should be going now," she said formally, as though she'd come over for afternoon tea. "I've enjoyed talking to you, Spence."

I shifted awkwardly. "Well, any time."

"Sometimes, sitting here, I talk to you in my mind and I have the feeling you hear me. Or at least you say things back and they're good, helpful things."

"That's just your imagination," I told her.

"I guess so." She looked earnest. "But it seems real."

111

Then she turned and started off down the street.

"Hey, Taff," I called, loping after her. "Let me drive you back, okay? It's so late and all—"

"It's just a few blocks," she said. "If people see the car, they might be suspicious."

The streets around here are well lit, but the idea of her wandering around alone made me nervous. I watched till she'd moved out of sight and then went upstairs. Then I realized I should've said something to her about coming here. What if my grandparents caught her at it? My grandfather would have a fit! I wondered how many times she'd done it. It gave me a spooky feeling, thinking of Taffy sitting in the swing and watching me at the window.

The one good effect seeing Taffy had was to make me almost forget about Audrey. She came back into my mind as I was brushing my teeth, but I pushed her away again.

## 11

A couple of days later when I went for my second donation a terrible thing happened. I just couldn't get in the mood. It was because of Audrey. Every time I'd start thinking of what I usually did to get excited—some woman or girl lying there, waiting for me—the girl would turn into Audrey and she'd start getting angry and parts of our fight would zap back into my mind. I sat there almost half an hour, really ashamed and embarrassed. Usually it takes me five minutes, ten at most. I tried thinking of Emmy Lou and making out with her, but that made me think of Taffy in her white nightgown. Oh, Christ. Here I pride myself on my willpower, and so many times I can get horny when it's the last thing in the world I want. Now every sexy thought I had would change into something completely unsexy in one second. But I knew if I left the room without being able to do it, I was finished.

Then I decided that anything that worked would be okay. Before I always tried to make my thoughts connect, like a story, to why I was there. But this time I imagined myself with Audrey, only it was more like a rape, almost. She was angry, but I just made her fuck me anyway, even though she was yelling and trying to kick me off. Still, even though it finally worked, I didn't leave feeling good the way I usually do. I felt crummy. For one thing, my sperm count probably wasn't as high as it should be. If I was an honest person, I'd go to them and tell them what happened. That same secretary was there, typing, when I came out. I put the sample down. She didn't say anything about how long I'd been in there.

That night Rob said he'd come over for a pizza and would sleep over, since my grandparents were still away. I hadn't seen him since the time we'd driven up to get him a room. He's working at a MacDonald's this summer, the same one he was at last summer, but this time he has the night shift, so he doesn't get off till eleven. I'd picked the pizza up at the place down the block.

"Boy, I'll never eat a hamburger again, after this summer," he said. "I can't even stand the smell anymore."

We ate in the kitchen on some paper plates my grandmother left. She knows I'm not too good about cleaning up when she's away.

"I'm beginning to get excited about college," Rob said, opening another beer. "It didn't seem that real before, but now that it's August and I've got a room, it feels like it'll really happen."

"I'll just be in the dorm," I said, "but I know what you mean."

He looked around. "Did you have that girl over, the

114

one you took bowling, now that your grandparents are away?"

I shook my head. "We broke up."

"How come?"

"Well, she was sort of a nymphomaniac."

"Oh." Rob looked thoughtful. "I've read about that, but I never actually met one. The girls I've known have been mainly in the other direction."

"It's not that good if you feel she just thinks of you as some kind of hulk, if she's just desperate for a guy," I belched. Anchovies and beer always make me do that.

"Why was she desperate, if she was so good-looking?" Rob wanted to know.

"Maybe because she was divorced." Just then the phone rang. I hoped it wasn't Audrey. It wasn't. It was Roxanne.

"Hi, Spence, how're you doing?"

"I'm okay," I said.

"Did you hear from Great-Grandma yet? She sent me two postcards."

"Yeah, I got a few, too."

"Hey, listen, I've got some great new records. Why don't you come over and hear them?"

"Okay," I said reluctantly.

"When? When're you going to come?"

"I—I'm not sure. . . . Listen, Roxanne? I've got this friend over now. Could I call you back some other time?"

"Is it a girl?" she asked excitedly. "Do you have a girl over?"

"No, it's just Rob, my friend."

"Oh." She sounded disappointed. "Well, have fun anyway."

Willa had invited me over for sometime when Grandma and Grandpa were away, but I'd forgotten about it. When I went back to the kitchen, Rob was lugging this huge bag of garbage out to the back. "What're you doing?"

"Don't you even take garbage out?" he said. "It stinks in there."

"They don't pick it up till Friday."

"Still, man, you can't live like a pig. Here, help me."

I helped him carry the bag out to the back, where we have a big wooden holder for our garbage bags. As we were stuffing it in, I looked up and saw Taffy in the swing. Actually, I didn't see *her* so much. I just saw the swing moving back and forth. Rob stretched. "Boy, what a beautiful night."

"It's supposed to rain," I said nervously. I didn't want Rob seeing Taffy over there.

"Doesn't look like it." He looked up at the sky, which was covered with stars. "Let's sit outside a little."

"I'm getting pretty tired," I said.

"Already? It's not even midnight."

"I got up really early."

"Okay, well, I'll be in in a minute. I just want to sit out here awhile."

The swing was still moving. "Listen," I said. "I'll open the window upstairs. It'll be just like sitting outside."

He looked at me, puzzled. "You have a nice garden back here," he commented. "Does your grandmother still grow tomatoes?"

"Yeah," I said, "but they're not ripe yet."

116

"How about raspberries? Remember how she used to make homemade raspberry jam?"

"Actually, I think we have some inside." I pulled his arm. "Let's go in. We can have some on crackers."

Rob got up. The mention of food is about the only surefire thing to get him moving. "You still have that swing," he said.

"Right."

What was strange was that it was still swinging, but he didn't seem to notice. I turned and started in to the house, and a second later, he followed. I knew what I ought to do was tell Rob about Taffy, but somehow it didn't seem right. I also wished I'd said something firmer to her the other night about not coming around.

Once we were in the house, I felt better. I got out the raspberry jam and Rob gobbled up some crackers, jam, and milk. By then it was past midnight. On the way to the bathroom, I looked out and the swing wasn't moving anymore. I figured Taffy'd gone home. Rob slept on the floor on my air mattress like he usually does. He tends to fall asleep pretty quickly. Just before he did, he said, "I hope I meet a good girl, someone I really like the first week of college."

"You know three already," I reminded him.

"They weren't my type. More like friends."

"What's your type?"

He was silent awhile. "Well, maybe a combination of Edina and a little bit like Taffy, Linc's Taffy, I mean. I could always talk to her. She used to tell me about how she had a crush on you, but I knew you weren't that interested, so . . ."

"Maybe I made a mistake," I said. "I could've gone with her instead of Emmy."

"Yeah, but then you might've ended up with a kid."

"True . . . but I think I would've used something, no matter what she said."

Rob rolled. "I guess people get carried away sometimes . . . so they say."

So they say! Shit. Two seconds after that he was asleep, and I was lying there, curled in a knot, thinking about Audrey. I wish I'd never met her. I wish June had gone in to get those tickets herself. But then I started thinking back on the good part of what'd happened between us, not just the time by the river, but the drives in her car, talking with her. Usually with girls I like them or don't like them completely. I don't have any indecision about it. But with Audrey I felt both all the time. Even lying there, I almost felt like I wanted to see her again, if only to apologize about that remark about her picking someone up on the way home.

I wonder if she did. Maybe she did! Maybe there's nothing to apologize about! Not that I'm going to. But like she said, she probably meets a lot of guys who put the make on her. I think it was more than just physical attraction. Most of my sisters went to bed with their husbands before they got married. All except June. She said one thing she liked about Silas was he wasn't that pushy about sex.

Rob slept late in the morning. I went jogging and, even after I got back, he was still asleep. I showered and started the coffee going. I was glad he'd taken the garbage out. It did smell a lot better. While I was frying some eggs, the phone rang. There've been a lot

118

of messages for my grandmother since I guess she didn't tell everyone she was going away.

"Hello?" I said.

"Spence? It's Audrey."

"Oh . . . hi." I started feeling tense again when I heard her voice.

"I hate the thing of bearing grudges and saying things I don't mean. So I wanted to apologize about the other night. You weren't ready. I guess I sensed that, but I sort of got carried away."

"Well that's okay," I said, twisting the phone cord. "I got carried away, too."

"The fact is, I don't even *like* good-looking guys," she went on. "You just seemed like an unusual person to me."

I hesitated. "I didn't mean what I said about you just being . . . you know, about picking someone up on the way home."

"Actually, I did. He was cute."

I was silent.

"Hey, it was a joke. Okay?"

I smiled tensely. "I'm frying these eggs."

"Not as good as mine, I bet," she said. "Why don't you let me come over and fix you dinner now that your folks are away?"

"Sure, that'd be good."

"How's Friday?"

I said Friday was fine.

I was in the middle of eating eggs and toast when Rob came downstairs, yawning. "I always sleep really well at your house," he said. "I don't know why. Ever since my parents split, I don't sleep well either at his house *or* her house. I guess I'm always

119

worried that she's in there crying, or that he's making out with some asshole half his age."

"Maybe they'll get back together," I suggested.

"It looks doubtful. He says he wants to start all over, you know, have a new family, the works."

"How about your mom?"

"She just wants to kill him. . . . It'd be good if she'd find somebody. Then she might stop worrying about me all the time."

"My grandmother worries about me."

"I think my mother does it more," Rob said, "on account of my being an only child."

"I'm *like* an only child," I said. "My sisters being so much older and me being the only boy."

Rob threw two eggs in the pan. "Right . . . there are similarities. Man, I'm starving. Aren't you glad I got that garbage out of here? How can you live like that?"

"You're a good influence," I said, grinning.

He deposited the eggshells in the new garbage bag. "I'm a very neat person. My father says I'm going to drive whoever I marry out of her skull."

# 12

Friday, the day Audrey said she'd come over, it poured rain all day. I didn't do all that much. Mercer had some plastering job that he said I could help with. After that I stopped over at Willa's and listened to Roxanne's new album. Despite everything, I was glad Audrey was coming over. With my grandparents away, it's true I have total freedom, but there's also no structure to things. I like structure. Plus, I really am a lousy cook. Partly it's just laziness, but also even when I follow a simple recipe, something seems to go wrong. Maybe my heart isn't in it. So when I saw Audrey pull up in her car, and then trot up the walk in her yellow slicker, carrying a big shopping bag in one hand, I felt good.

I helped her carry the stuff into the kitchen. She looked all around. I'd forgotten she'd never been at my house before. "It's nice," she said. "It's such a huge house! How does your grandmother manage?"

"I don't know. I guess she just cleans one room at a time." I never thought about it that much.

"Does she work?"

I shook my head. "Well, she had to raise me and my four sisters. And now, she has to look after my grandfather. He's more trouble than kids."

"How come?" She slapped a big steak on the table. My favorite, I could eat steak every day.

"He's almost eighty."

"Boy, that I will never do," Audrey said. "Spend my whole life just catering to some man."

"Well, she loves him, I guess."

"Love!" Audrey snorted. "That's messed up the minds and lives of more women than anything you can name."

"How about the lives of men?" I said teasingly.

"Men are more laid back. It's like they have this little self-interested calculating side that never turns off. Women just go hog-wild if they fall for someone." She looked around. "Hey, I need a good heavy pan. . . . Is steak okay? I thought I'd stick to the basics. I got green beans and a nice french bread and some wine."

"I don't drink wine that much," I said. My mouth was starting to water already. I got her out a pan and a smaller pot for the beans.

"Okay, well, suit yourself. I'll just have a glass or two. I'm not going to force it on you."

I thought we'd eat in the kitchen the way I usually do, but when Audrey saw we had a dining room, she started setting up in there. Usually my grandmother saves the dining room for special occasions like Thanksgiving. It's a long shiny table with a buffet on the side.

122

I have to admit, it was a stupendous meal. Despite Audrey's far-out convictions about men and women, she can definitely cook well. I told her that. She grinned. "Yeah, I'm good at basics . . . don't try me on fancy stuff. And you know, retrograde as it may be, I like feeding men. Isn't that awful? Maybe it's some primitive thing, but they always look so pleased and satisfied."

That's exactly how I felt. I'd had two glasses of wine and it made me feel warm and relaxed.

We looked at each other. I realize now there's one problem with having had sex with someone, unless it's been awful or they decide they never want to see you again. It's that, no matter what you're doing, just having dinner or seeing a movie, you're partly, maybe way beneath the surface, thinking about the possibility of doing it. You just see them differently than you would otherwise.

Audrey must've been having the same thought. She reached out and touched my hand. "We don't have to do anything, Spence, not if you don't want. I just wanted to come over here and be with you."

"Right." If she was Rob, we could just watch TV or talk. I tried to pretend it was like that, casual, no fuss.

"Why don't I make some coffee? Or does it keep you up?"

"No, I'd like some." I followed her into the kitchen. I kept trying not to look at her body, but it was pretty impossible.

We had coffee, but I just couldn't keep up my end of the conversation. Audrey was telling me something about her mother and every once in a while, she'd look at me and I'd try and look like I'd been listening.

Once she leaned forward and waved her hand in front of me. "Hey!" she said. "Where are you?"

I grinned dumbly. "I don't know what we should do."

She smiled. "Whatever we want."

"I guess I don't know *what* I want."

Audrey looked thoughtful. "I think maybe we shouldn't, Spence. Really. Not that I don't want to. But I think afterward you'd feel bad again, don't you think?"

"Yeah, probably," I admitted. In my mind I kept going over to her and putting my arms around her and running my hands down her back. It was like mentally we were doing it and physically we were sitting there, having coffee and talking about whether her mother should marry her boyfriend, if he ever got his divorce. "Not that he's going to," Audrey said. "I think it's all a pipe dream. But even if he did, what would she have? This greasy guy with sideburns who drives a '76 Ford and is impotent half the time. My mother's such a sweetie. Why can't she get someone better than that?"

"I don't know," I said. I was having a little trouble breathing. Also, I knew Audrey could tell everything I was feeling.

Finally she got up and put her arms around me. "Hon, this is too complicated for you, isn't it? Why don't I go home? We can talk in the morning.

Part of me wanted to just yank her upstairs, but I said, "Right, that might be better."

After she left, I felt really lousy. What's wrong with me? Here's someone I finally like who seems to like me. I felt all wired up and confused. I always thought of myself as someone with high ideals who could control their thoughts as well as their actions, but lately I act like some kind of wind-up toy going this way, that way. Just to do something, to try and get my mind off Audrey, I cleaned up in the kitchen. I actually washed the pans—usually I just leave them for the next day. But after that was over, I still felt pretty much the same. I even thought of calling her up and telling her I'd changed my mind. Instead I went out in the garden. The swing was empty. I went over and sat down in it and sat there, taking deep breaths of the night air. I closed my eyes.

"Hi, Spence." I opened my eyes with a start. There was Taffy, sitting opposite me.

I sat up straight and looked at her, alarmed. She must have come along while I was dozing.

"Were you waiting for me?"

"No, uh, I was just . . . I felt like being outside."

"It's such a beautiful night, isn't it?" She leaned back on the swing and gazed at me dreamily.

"Yeah, it's nice."

Taffy kept looking at me. "This is the only part of the day when I feel alive. The rest of the day I feel like I'm dead, like I'm just doing things and they're not real and I'm not real, the baby's not real. . . . I just started thinking of that today. I looked down at the baby and he looked so—like a doll, not like a real baby."

"Well, he's real, all right," I said.

"Right." She just kept staring at me in a way that made me uncomfortable. "There was a girl here before, wasn't there?"

"How do you know?"

"I was over by the bushes. I didn't want to visit you

125

till she went home. Was it the girl you took bowling with us?"

"Yeah . . ." I sat forward. "Listen, Taffy, I really think you better stop coming over here like this. It's not right. You shouldn't be doing it."

Taffy's big eyes widened. "Why?"

"What's it for?" I said. "You have a family. You have a husband."

"No," Taffy said, looking down. "I don't, really. Everything I have just seems real, but it's not. Linc isn't really my husband. He doesn't want to be and I don't think of him as my husband. I think of you as my husband, Spence."

"But I'm not," I said, alarmed. "That's not healthy, pretending like that."

She looked off again, twisting her wispy hair around her finger. "It's true in a way."

"No, it's not! It's not true in *any* way!"

"Remember when we were in the eighth grade and we went to that State Fair together and you got this box of Crackerjacks and the prize in it was a ring and it didn't fit you, so you said, 'You take it, Taffy,' and you put it on my finger?"

I vaguely remembered, just about our going there, not about the ring. "That was when we were just thirteen!"

"When you were putting it on, I thought: I love you. And I still do. I still love you, Spence. And I always will, even if you marry the girl you brought bowling with us, no matter what." Her words were all breathless and strung together.

"I'm not going to marry her," I said nervously.

Taffy's eyes shone. "I knew you wouldn't. She's

just for sex, just to get experience. I knew you didn't really love her."

I took a deep breath. "Taffy, listen, I can't handle all this. It makes me feel guilty. Linc's my friend. And I don't think it's that good for you either. You're pretending. You're making a game out of our lives."

There was a moment of silence. "I know it's not real," Taffy whispered.

"Then why do it? What's the point?"

"Because I hate the way things really are! I hate my life!" Suddenly Taffy flung herself into my arms. She started crying.

I held her in my arms, patting her. "Taffy, don't cry. Please."

"You don't have to come out and talk to me," she murmured. "Just let me be here. I'm not hurting you. Am I?"

I don't know if it was because of getting all stirred up earlier with Audrey or just because Taffy was clinging to me in her soft nightgown (even though she had her windbreaker on over it), but I suddenly felt terribly attracted to her. "Taffy, please don't come over here anymore," I pleaded. "I can't take it. It's not right."

"I want you so much," she said. "I think of you every time we make love. I always have."

I felt like everything in the garden was spinning around. I put my hand out to touch the wood of the swing.

"I'd give my life for you," Taffy went on, her breath soft on my neck. "I really would. I'd do anything you want."

The next part is the worst thing I've ever done. With Audrey at least I didn't think it was bad till it was over.

But with Taffy I knew every second I was doing something terrible, that I'd never forgive myself for it if I lived to be a hundred. But I made love to her anyway. It was like it started happening and halfway through I felt like I was comforting her and telling her to stop, and when it became something else, my mind was so blurry I couldn't think. After it was over, Taffy clung to me, almost the way she had before. "I wish I could die now," she said.

I almost wished I could, too, but not in the way she meant it. I tried to talk in a gentle, quiet way. I didn't want her to get all upset again. "We shouldn't have done this. It was a terrible thing."

"No, it was wonderful," Taffy said, her eyes shining. "It was the most wonderful thing that ever happened to me."

"We can't ever do it again," I said intensely. "You've got to stop coming here. Will you promise me that?"

I thought she would protest, but she said, "I promise . . . I'll do anything you want. Do you want to never see me again?"

I stroked her shoulder. "No, of course I want to see you again, but I want . . . I want you to be happy. I'll be going off to college in a few weeks and—"

"You'll meet girls there, you'll be a doctor, you'll have a wonderful life," Taffy said in a kind of monotone.

"I'll just have a regular life," I said. "It won't be that wonderful."

Taffy was looking up at the stars. "Just think— somewhere right now there's some girl who one day will marry you, Spence, and she doesn't even know. She's probably worried about some regular, ordinary thing, and she doesn't know one day her whole life will be different! One day she'll be the happiest person on earth!"

Every word she said made me feel guiltier. It ought to feel good to have someone idealize you that much, but it's a burden too. I sat up. "Taff, maybe you should go home now, do you think? It's really late."

"Right, I'll go home now." She looked up at me. "Did you, was it . . . do you feel happy now, Spence?"

"Yeah, sure, I feel happy." I just wanted to get her home and safe.

I stood at the door and watched her drift off down the street. I felt worse than I'd ever felt in my life. Happy? I felt like some kind of monster! How could I do that? What's wrong with me? I must be crazy. When I got back into the house, the phone was ringing. I lifted it up. "Hello?"

It was Linc. "Hey, listen, Spence, I'm sorry to bother you so late at night, but Taffy's disappeared."

I went cold. "Disappeared?"

"I woke up and she wasn't there. I don't know. I feel like maybe she's flipping out. She's been acting really strange lately. You haven't seen her, have you?"

"No, no," I stammered. "I haven't."

"I think maybe she's crazy," he said. "She's acting so weird."

"She's okay," I said. "Don't worry about it."

"Where is she then? It's past one."

"She's probably just decided to take a walk."

"A walk? At this hour of night? . . . Oh, Christ, there she is. I see her, coming up the steps. Listen, I'll talk to you tomorrow or something. Thanks a lot."

I hung up the phone. Thanks a lot for fucking my

wife. Linc's my friend. Maybe not my best friend, but still my friend. Okay, maybe he doesn't always treat Taffy that well, but that doesn't excuse what I just did. I got into bed and tried to think of something completely different, like whether my grandparents were having a good time on their vacation. But that didn't work. It was so ironical. If I'd done it with Audrey, like she wanted to, nothing would have happened. She might've stayed over, and I wouldn't have even known Taffy was there.

Finally I did fall asleep, but I had weird complicated dreams of being back in high school and trying to find a classroom that seemed not to be there. It was like I wouldn't graduate unless I found the room, but no one knew where it was. I woke up, sweating, at eight in the morning. The sun was blazing in the window. I felt a lot better.

Only the next time the phone rang it was my grandmother, calling to tell me my grandfather had died.

# 13

"He was just sitting there in the beach chair, and all I did was go into the ocean for a minute, just to test it, and when I got back, it had happened. He looked just the way he had before, but his eyes didn't open." My grandmother started to cry again. "Oh, I shouldn't have gone into the ocean! Why did I do that?"

All my sisters were over at the house, trying to comfort my grandmother and take care of her. "Gran, he was almost eighty and you know he'd had high blood pressure for years," Willa said. "He lived a long and happy life."

"Did he?" My grandmother looked pleadingly at all of us.

"Of course he did," June said. I think she felt bad because it had happened while they were on a vacation she'd paid for. "And you were a wonderful wife for him, the best anyone ever had."

At that my grandmother started to cry again. "I wasn't," she said. "I wasn't a good wife."

Lizzie was patting her hand. "Of course you were. Grandpa adored you."

"I wasn't smart enough," my grandmother said. "I couldn't even do the crossword puzzle with him! I never knew a single word. When he wanted me to read an article in the paper, I just pretended. I couldn't understand what those articles were about. I bossed him around. I made him do things he didn't want."

"Gran, listen to me," Willa said. "You tried to get him to do things that were good for him. Like this trip. You wanted him to get some fun out of life."

Personally I doubt my grandfather ever got fun out of anything. Or, if he did, he probably wouldn't have let on about it.

"All he talked about, all week, was wanting to get home again," my grandmother said. "He kept saying, 'Why are we here?' He just wanted to get back to see all of you again." Her eye fell on me. "He was so proud of all of you."

My grandmother always said that, but I sure never could see it. My grandfather never came to my high school graduation, even. He claimed he wasn't feeling that well. Even the day I heard I had a scholarship to college, he just shoved the letter in my face and said, "There!" as though I'd done something terrible. My grandmother claimed it was because he was going to miss me so much when I went away! What was he going to miss? He never talked to me when I was around, except to make fun of me or make strange remarks.

I know sometimes people say that it isn't till after people are dead that you really appreciate them. Or that you suddenly wish you had tried harder to communicate with them or told them you loved them.

I'm sorry to say this, but that isn't true with my grandfather. First, I did try to communicate with him about a million times and it just never worked. He either acted like I wasn't there or as though I was some peculiar unnecessary person who he had to have meals with and give money to occasionally. I remember most the summer I had this job in Maine, where he grew up and lived till he was twelve. I'd never been there before and it really is a beautiful place. I wrote him all these long, excited letters about what I was doing, sending color snapshots of beautiful scenes, and he never even replied. The only way I even knew the letters had arrived was my grandmother would mention it in *her* letters. I don't think once in his whole *life* he wrote me a letter. My grandmother would write and sometimes, at the very bottom, he'd add, "and Grandpa" or "Margaret's said it all." How *could* she say it all? Didn't he have anything to say about anything? Any thought or reaction that wasn't hers? I used to feel like he was some kind of ventriloquist's dummy and if my grandmother hadn't pretended he was alive, he wouldn't have been. At the dinner table she'd tell him things and, even if he didn't respond any more than he did with me, she'd act as though he had and keep right on talking.

Meanwhile, while I was sitting in the back of the room, my sisters were still clustered around my grandmother, offering to send over food or have her come stay with them. My grandmother sat there, a little dazed, like she was only half listening to them. Then suddenly she said, "But did he love me?"

There was a moment of silence.

"Of course he loved you," Carnie said. "How can you doubt that?"

"He loved you to *pieces*," June said. "If you left the room, it was like the sun went down."

"You were the only reason he lived so long," Lizzie put in. "Without you, he would have just given up the ghost years ago."

My grandmother was picking at some threads on the chair. "He never said it," she whispered. "He never told me he did."

Lizzie let out a snort. "Oh, men are like that, Gran. They never say anything. You've got to read between the lines."

"Not all men," Carnie said, blushing.

Willa was drinking a can of beer. "It's true," she said gloomily. "When Jake asked me to marry him, I said, 'Do you love me?' and he said, 'Why else would I be asking you?'"

I wonder if my grandfather did love my grandmother. If he didn't, it would sure be unfair, considering how much she did for him. "I think he loved you," I said, just to say something.

My grandmother's face got that warm, melting expression it often does when she looks at me. "You were the apple of his eye, Spence," she said. "He told me over and over how proud he was to have a grandson. That meant so much to him."

I tried not to sound sarcastic. "He never said it to me."

"He just wasn't a talkative person," my grandmother observed. "He kept it all inside. I think that's why he had high blood pressure."

"Actions speak louder than words," Carnie said.

"He was a family man," my grandmother went on. "I knew that from the day I laid eyes on him. He wanted a family more than anything."

134

She sighed. "Well, I suppose you never know if you've done the right thing."

"Gran, look," June said, stroking her. "Grandpa was a difficult person, moody, taciturn. You can't blame yourself for that. He was what he was."

My grandmother looked horrified. "Moody? No! *I* had moods. He was always so calm."

"What I mean is," June said softly, "he was lucky to get you, *darn* lucky."

"*I* was lucky," my grandmother exclaimed. "I was the lucky one."

Turning, June went off into the kitchen. For some reason I followed her. She opened the refrigerator door, took out a Coke, and slammed the door shut. Then she looked at me, her hazel eyes blazing. "He was so awful about Silas!" she said. "I just can't forgive him about that. He called him a no-good, just because he fell in love with someone."

"He was prejudiced," I said. "Against everybody and everything."

"He was a bastard," June said. "Let's face it."

"You're not kidding." I felt really relieved at having someone else in the family say that aloud.

"She waited on him hand and *foot*, like a lackey! She should've just socked him in the jaw a couple of times."

I laughed. It was pretty hard to imagine a scene like that. "Why'd you spend all that money sending them on a trip?" I asked.

"It was for Gran," June said with a hopeless shrug. "I wanted her to have some fun."

I picked up some potato chips that were out on the counter. "He never even came to my graduation," I said. "Even after I asked him especially."

"He never did *anything*," June said. "He didn't visit me once the whole time I was a nun. Okay, so he disapproved. Gran disapproved more, but *she* came."

"So, how come she loved him so much?"

"Women are like that," June said wearily. "They're crazy when it comes to love."

That made me think of Taffy and that awful night in the garden. I'd almost completely put it out of my mind. And I thought of what Audrey said about women going hog-wild when they love someone. Taffy's loving me didn't make any more sense than my grandmother's loving my grandfather.

June was drinking her Coke straight from the bottle. "It's too bad you never knew Daddy," she said. "You would've loved him. He was so excited when Mom had you, after all of us girls. He used to toss you up in the air, and you'd laugh and laugh. Do you remember that?"

I shook my head. I always feel awful when my sisters talk about my parents, partly because, being so much older than me, they remember so much more. It's like I never had parents. I don't remember anything.

Finally, at around midnight, all my sisters cleared out. In his will my grandfather had said he wanted to be cremated and didn't want any kind of service. He said he just wanted his ashes sprinkled over Lake Paloma, where he used to go fishing sometimes. My grandmother asked if I'd go with her when she went to sprinkle the ashes.

"Sure," I said, putting my arm around her. "When do you want to go?"

"Let's wait for a beautiful day," my grandmother said. "Oh, it's so helpful having you around, Spence.

You're such a comfort. Now you're the man of the family, responsible for all of us females. How does that feel?"

I guess I don't look at it that way exactly, since my sisters are all so much older and living on their own. "I'll take care of you," I said, just because I thought it was what she wanted to hear.

"I know you will," my grandmother said. "And you know, maybe, when we're sprinkling the ashes, you could say a poem, the way you used to at school. Would you do that?"

I nodded.

My grandmother was carrying glasses back into the kitchen. "I wonder what I should do about the house," she said. "It seems so big now. . . . And soon you'll be off to school, I'll be here all alone." At the thought of that her face started to crumple.

"I'll come home weekends," I promised.

"It's such a big house," my grandmother whimpered. "Maybe I'll get a little apartment somewhere, just one room or two, pitch out all this stuff."

"You could move in with Willa," I said. "She has a big house."

"No," my grandmother said firmly. "I don't want that. That leads to trouble, living with your children. I can manage on my own perfectly well. I'm not *that* old, you know, Spence."

"You could get married again," I said.

To my surprise my grandmother laughed. "Could I? You think someone would have me? Now what I *should* do, this time around, is get me a younger man, someone lively who loves dancing. That's the fashion, you know."

"It is?"

"Who knows," my grandmother said. "You have to let life happen to you, good or bad. That's what I said when Eleanor died. I thought my life was over. I even thought of doing away with myself. But then I thought of the girls and you and . . . well, I didn't."

My grandmother never struck me as the type to have such gloomy thoughts. She always seemed so cheerful, ready to cope with anything.

"Were my parents happy together?"

My grandmother beamed. "Oh yes! Goodness, it gave me such a kick to be with them. Kell just adored your mother. I think he'd had girlfriends, being so good looking, but no serious ones. Once he met her, that was it."

"I don't even remember them," I said. "I wish I could."

"I wish you could, too," my grandmother said. "You know, Spence, I look at you sometimes and you look so much like your father, my heart just stops. He had so many plans for you. He knew you'd be a good athlete. He always said, 'Look at his feet!' You had huge feet, even as a baby."

"I still do."

My grandmother sighed. "Well, what's done is done, but you know, ever since then I've never felt quite the same way about the Lord. I go to church and I guess you'd call me a believer, but I hope He has a damn good explanation for this . . ." Her voice broke.

I hugged her. I love my grandmother. She's not like a mother, but she's a good person and she's done her best. I hope she'll be okay without my grandfather. She's so used to looking after someone, and I'll be off to college soon.

The next day I went over to Rob's house. I'd told him about my grandfather and he said he was sorry.

His father said he was sorry, too. "How's your grandmother taking it?" he asked.

"Oh, I think she'll be okay," I said. "Maybe she'll marry again."

Rob's father looked up. "How old is she?"

"Seventy-three."

"Sounds perfect for you, Dad," Rob said.

Rob's father snorted. "He thinks I'm a dirty old man just because I like younger women. I'm just being practical. When I'm old and decrepit, they can look after me, cater to my needs."

Rob looked disgusted.

"Women like men who are mature, wise, genial," he went on.

"Look, I'm not stopping you," Rob said irritably. "Marry one of them if you feel like it."

"I'll do as I see fit," his father said stiffly, then walked off, looking annoyed.

"What a jerk," Rob said. "Anyone who'd marry him would have to be off her rocker. Hey, listen, did Linc call you?"

My heart started beating fast. "A couple of days ago . . . why?"

"It sounds like Taffy is acting a little strange. He thought maybe we should go over and visit with them."

My stomach tightened. "I—I don't know," I said. "I don't think I can."

Rob looked puzzled. "Why not?"

"I just—I don't want to see her."

"I thought you liked her. She always liked you."

Most things that've happened to me, important

things, I've told Rob about. But the incident with Taffy made me feel so ashamed. I didn't even want to tell him. "I can't explain it," I said inadequately.

"Well, I promised I'd go over there," Rob said. "I said you'd come along."

"I'll drop you off," I said. "I—uh—promised my grandmother I'd stick around the house."

That was the perfect excuse. Rob nodded understandingly. "Oh, yeah, I forgot."

I drove Rob to Linc's parents' house after we'd had lunch. I was hoping they'd be inside, but instead, Taffy was out in front, working in the garden. When she saw me, her face lit up. "I didn't know you were coming," she said.

"I—I can't stay," I said. "My grandfather died, and I have to get back to be with my grandmother."

"Oh . . . I'm so sorry, Spence. When did that happen? He was such a sweet person."

"It was just heart failure," I explained, seeing Linc walking out of the house.

Linc came up behind Taffy and called out, "Hi, come on in."

"His grandfather died," Taffy said half turning. "He died of heart failure."

"He was almost eighty," I went on, trying to look away from Taffy. The expression in her eyes made me nervous.

"Is your grandmother all right?" Taffy said anxiously. "She must be so upset."

"She's okay. . . . She's taking it pretty well."

Taffy put her hand on my arm. "I'll go over to see her. She must be so sad. She loved him so much."

"Not now," Linc said. He folded his arms. "Better wait until she's feeling better."

"We're sprinkling his ashes over Lake Paloma," I said. "That's what he wanted."

Taffy had left her hand on my arm. It lay there warmly. "That's a very beautiful thing to do," she said. "I'd like to have that done when I die."

Linc's face darkened. "Taff, you're not going to die for a long time. You don't have to start planning your service now."

She looked at him angrily. "Why not? I can plan it whenever I want."

Rob had gotten out of the car and was standing there silently. I wasn't sure if they even saw him. "Rob's going to stay awhile," I said. "I have to head off."

"Tell your grandmother I'll come to see her soon," Taffy said. Whenever she looked at me, I seemed to see her face the way it had looked that night in the garden with the moonlight passing over it, her hair looking silver and soft. Sometimes I feel like I could fall in love with Taffy and that makes me feel sick and nervous with dread.

I drove off, relieved that I had the excuse of my grandmother to get away. Ironically, when I got home, my grandmother wasn't even there. Probably she was out visiting some of her friends, the ones who'd called while she was away. I wondered if she would sell the house. Where would she put all the junk she'd accumulated over the years? I guess I'll take most of my stuff to college, but there's so much furniture and dishes, rugs, pictures.

I know one thing: I'll be glad to get away.

# 14

For weeks after my grandfather died, my grandmother mostly stayed around the house. Sometimes her friends would come to visit her, or she'd write letters to the ones that lived far away. She didn't talk any more about selling the house. My sisters seemed to think that was good. "She shouldn't make too many changes right off the bat," Willa said.

"It's good you're there," June added. "It's good for her to have a man around."

"I'll be leaving in a couple of weeks," I reminded them. I didn't want to feel guilty about that. I'd been looking forward so long to getting out of the house, starting a new life at college.

"Oh, by then she'll be fine," Carnie predicted. I think she sensed some of what I was feeling.

"I just meant for now," June said. "You're a great comfort to her, Spence."

"She has all her friends," I pointed out.

"She'll be fine," Lizzie said. "We're all worrying

143

about her like she was a baby, like she couldn't cope without a man. You know what I bet? I bet she'll have a terrific life now, travel, do lots of things she always wanted to while Grandpa was alive but couldn't."

"I'll come home weekends to see her," I promised.

But Carnie said, "Don't go on a guilt trip, hon. You go off, have a fine year. We're all here. We'll check in on her."

Actually, my grandmother seemed fine to me. The only thing that got me worried a little was the amount of time she spent going over old photo albums. I'd come home and she'd be sitting in the living room with dozens of photos spread out around her on the table. She claimed she wanted to sort them out, paste in the ones she liked and maybe discard the rest. But, even though the pot of glue was beside her, I never saw her do any pasting or sorting. She'd just look at them and start in reminiscing about the past.

One day I came home from being with Audrey and found that my grandmother had taken out a big photo of my grandfather and propped it up in one of the armchairs. "I'd forgotten all about this one," she exclaimed. "Isn't he handsome? That was taken just about when I met him. We'd had a fight once, I don't remember about what, and he said he wanted me to have that photo to look at. It was true, every time I'd start to get mad at him about anything, I'd look at that photo and I'd just melt."

I looked at the photo. There was old Omar in his marine uniform, his mouth set in a kind of half grin. The photo was of him in half profile and he did have good features, I guess, a straight nose and thin eyebrows. Of course, it was one of those official photos that're designed to make people look good.

"Yeah, well . . ." I couldn't think of what to say. I'd never tell my grandmother any of the negative things I felt about my grandfather, but I couldn't get myself to lie either.

"He had such a sensitive face!" she went on. "His eyes! People said he was silent, but I just had to look in his eyes and I could tell everything he was feeling. He was a man of deep feelings. You didn't know that, Spence, but he was."

"Sure," I said uncomfortably.

From then on whenever I came into the living room there would be the photo of my grandfather in the armchair. It was a nine by twelve, so it fit into the chair pretty well. My grandmother had even draped one of my grandfather's sweaters around the edge of it. When I asked her about that at dinner, she said, "I was afraid he might get cold."

"Gran, it's just a photo," I said. "How can it get cold?"

My grandmother sipped her tea thoughtfully. "Well, I know you may not believe this, Spence, but I think it's more than a photo. Or, at any rate, it's a photo with certain special powers."

My heart sank. "What kind of powers?" I said.

My grandmother's voice lowered. "The other day I was sitting there, leafing through the photos, sorting them and I just happened to look up, and his eyes glanced over at me and he almost smiled. It wasn't quite a smile. But about his eyes there was no doubt. He wasn't coming back, but he was telling me that he was there with me, in spirit."

I was silent.

"Tonight I want you to come in and see," she said. "You watch him and you'll see. Of course it may not

145

happen whenever we want it to. But if you look at him and think of him in a special way, it will."

"I don't want to," I said.

My grandmother looked hurt. "Please, Spence, I know you and Omar didn't always get along, but he loved you and he wants to know you loved him back. Just because he's not with us anymore in body, his spirit still needs that comfort." Her voice trembled.

My voice was a little shaky, too. "Gran, I don't believe in it! I can't!"

"Do it for me," she urged. "Just this once. I won't ask you again."

I hesitated. Then I thought how, after all, the point of this, was just that it was making my grandmother feel better. "Okay," I said.

After dinner she turned on a TV show my grandfather used to like to watch, *The Yellow Ribbon*. It's a Western and, ironically, when he was alive, my grandmother used to rail on about what a dumb show it was—it is!—and why didn't he even try something else. She never once, that I recall, watched it with him.

"Do I have to watch the show, too?" I said, trying not to sound impatient. It was as bad as some of those old John Wayne things.

"Just this once, honey," she said, patting my hand. "It's really not a bad show. I don't know why I had all those prejudices against it. Omar was right. It has all the values that are important in it—family loyalty, respect for women, men who act the way men should . . ."

I'm sorry, but to me it was about the dumbest show I've ever seen in my life. If that's the way men should act, according to my grandfather, then he had even

146

more screwed-up values than I thought. I just sat there restlessly, thinking about Audrey, not even really concentrating on the show.

Since my grandfather's death I've been seeing Audrey a lot. And we make love every chance we get, which is pretty often. I don't know what triggered the whole thing—Taffy acting so strange or the shock of my grandfather vanishing suddenly, but it's like all I want to do is be with Audrey. All I think about most of the day, no matter what else I'm doing, is her, her body, her expressions, the way her hands feel as she touches me. I still go to the Clinic, but it doesn't matter as much to me anymore. She's the only thing that matters.

"There!" my grandmother said suddenly, tugging my arm. "Did you see?"

"What?" I said, dragging my mind back from Audrey's expression as she looked up at me in the middle of making love.

"He smiled at you!" My grandmother looked really excited. "He's so happy you're watching the show with me. Look at him now, Spence. Maybe he'll do it again."

I looked at the photo of my grandfather. He looks so different from the way I remember him that I don't even feel I'm looking at him. "I don't see anything," I said.

What's weird about all this is that in every other way my grandmother is exactly the way she always was—practical, down to earth. She isn't even that religious and never was. So I can't figure out where this is coming from. It seems so unlike her.

My grandmother stood up and turned the TV off. "You know," she mused, "we could try another show

147

some night, but I feel as though, if he *is* here with us, it must be because he misses certain things about the real world."

I grinned. "Maybe they have prime time up where he is too. Celestial TV. You probably don't even have to turn it on."

My grandmother looked at me disapprovingly. "I don't believe in any of that," she said. "That's all superstition, all that talk of heaven and angels."

"But Gran," I said, "what you're doing is the same. You're just imagining he's part of some spirit world that doesn't exist either."

"Then why does he look at me?" my grandmother asked. "What does that mean?"

"I don't know." I thought it would be cruel to say straight out I thought she was imagining it.

My grandmother looked at me in exasperation. "Spence, do I strike you as the kind of person who would just make something like this up?"

I shook my head.

"I don't believe in it any more than you do," she said. "But there is no doubt in my mind that he is with us right this second. It's not that I want it, even. It's just a fact."

When I saw her the next evening, Audrey told me I should try and be more understanding. "She's grieving," she said. "It's her way. Everyone invents some way of coping with things that are unbearable. I felt like that when Mike and I split. Every time I even thought about it, I felt like someone had taken a knife and sliced me down the center."

She was lying naked next to me, and the warmth of her body, her smell, her skin seemed the only thing in life worth caring about, the only real thing. "You didn't do anything like this, did you?" I asked. "Imagining stuff that wasn't real?"

"No, but I'm not your grandmother's age. After all, she was married to him over fifty years. Think how long that is, how much of her life."

"If I died, would you act like that?" I asked her.

Audrey smiled at me in that teasing, soft way. "If you died now?"

"No, after fifty years. Say we'd been married fifty years—"

She laughed. "I'm not going to be married to anyone fifty years."

"Why not?"

"I couldn't take it, all that shit women have to put up with, all that groveling and lying."

"How about all the happy people?" I said. She sounds so cynical when she talks like that.

"What happy people? Where are they? Show me." She sat up, challenging me.

"My parents were happy," I said. "So were my grandparents. Or else, why would grandmother be doing all this?"

"She's inventing him," Audrey exclaimed. "Don't you see, Spence? She invented him while he was alive, and she's inventing him now. Maybe this is what she wanted all along. You always say how he never talked to her. Well, now she can talk and if he doesn't answer, she can explain it by saying he's not 'permitted' to by the spirit world or whatever. So it's less painful."

Suddenly, after the warmth and wonderfulness of our bodies connecting and melting into each other, I felt totally cut off from her. "I'm going to be happily married," I said.

"Sure you will," Audrey said, as though I were a child she was pampering.

But her voice cut through me, that almost mocking "sure you will." What I don't understand is this: When we're making love, Audrey acts like she thinks I'm the most wonderful person in the world. And you can't pretend about that. Rob lent me this book once, and it said women can't pretend with their bodies—they've got to really feel involved. On the one hand it's a relief to me that she never asks "do you love me?" or keeps going on about all that romance stuff the way most girls do. But at other times I don't understand exactly how she can go back and forth, moaning like she was going crazy and then making these detached, ironical remarks.

That evening I went up to my room while my grandmother was watching *The Yellow Ribbon*. I can't stand sitting in the same room while she and the photo watch the show. When I came down, Taffy was there, sitting on the couch, looking at the photo album with my grandmother. They both looked up as I came downstairs.

"Oh, Spence, look at the lovely bouquet Taffy brought me," my grandmother said, pointing to a bunch of wildflowers on the table. "Isn't it lovely?"

"Yeah, it's nice." I immediately felt uncomfortable seeing Taffy. She was wearing a pretty blue sundress and sandals and had makeup on, like she was out on a date.

"Your grandmother was telling me how she's been reading your grandfather all these poems to see which one he wants her to recite when she sprinkles his ashes into the lake," Taffy said. "I think that's such a nice idea."

"He never cared for poetry all that much," my grandmother said. "While he was alive, that is. But now he sits there and listens so happily. I suppose he's regretting he didn't listen more while he was alive." She looked at Taffy. "You know, Spence thinks this is all my imagination. He doesn't believe the photo is real."

Taffy looked surprised. "But you said you saw his eyes move."

"I know, several times . . . though not as much lately. I came in four times today and each time he was deliberately *not* looking at me. And at first I was hurt, but then I realized the problem was that Omar, in the photo, is thirty-three. So of course he expects *me* to be as young as I was when he was that age. He's probably thinking, 'Why is she so old and funny-looking?' "

"Oh, you don't look old, Mrs. Searles," Taffy said. "You look pretty."

My grandmother beamed. "You're such a sweet girl, Taffy. Look at you. As young and sweet as ever, and a mother already! Goodness. It's hard to believe."

"Yes," Taffy said sadly. "I know."

"Lincoln is a fine young man," she went on.

Taffy didn't say anything. She looked quickly over at me and then away again.

"It's so hard for women," my grandmother went on, "to find men who are worthy of them. I did, and so did my daughter. I'm so glad you did too, Taffy."

Taffy just kept staring at me with that downcast, pleading look that made my inside shrink. "Spence is the way all men should be," she said.

My grandmother chose to take that as a compliment. "Yes, he is, isn't he?" she said, looking at me proudly. "He's never given me one moment's anxiety

151

or worry. I hear all these stories from my friends about their grandsons—drugs, sex, what have you. And I've never worried about Spence for one moment."

"He has such high ideals," Taffy said, looking at me like I was a statue.

"Oh, he does!" my grandmother agreed. "Did you read that essay he wrote, on Values That Have Guided Me Throughout Life? That should have been in a magazine! I never read anything so well expressed, so fine."

"No," Taffy said. "I never did either. . . . I wish Spence was my husband."

At that my grandmother looked disconcerted. "Well, but you have a lovely husband," she said. "You have a husband *and* a baby."

Taffy just looked away. She looked over at the photo of my grandfather. Then a moment later she looked back. "He looked at me!" she said, her eyes round.

My grandmother got all excited. "Did he? When? Just now?"

"Just this very second." Taffy looked excited, too. She glanced over at me. "He looked right at me, Spence!"

"Now isn't that amazing?" my grandmother said. "Right as we were sitting here! You know what the explanation is? You're a pretty young girl, and Omar always had an eye for beauty. Not that I couldn't trust him, but he couldn't resist taking a peep at you, Taffy. . . . Now Spence, what do you think of that?" She looked triumphant.

I was sitting there feeling like the top of my head was going to blow off. "What do I think of *what*?" I said.

"Of Taffy seeing Omar's eyes move! How do you explain *that* away?" she asked sardonically.

"I think maybe you're both crazy," I said, trying to joke.

My grandmother turned to Taffy. "Well, at least we're *both* crazy! That's a great comfort to me because I was afraid Spencer thought it was just me."

Taffy smiled. "Maybe he thinks all women are crazy."

"Look, it's not—" I began.

But my grandmother interrupted. "Just tell me, Spence, what *is* your explanation? You have in this room with you two women whom the world, such as it is, considers intelligent and sane. Yet we *both* saw those eyes move."

Boy, did I wish I were away at college already or on another planet somewhere. I cleared my throat. "Well, I think you miss Grandpa," I said, "and you want him to be here still, and so you imagine he is because it makes you feel better."

"And how about Taffy?" my grandmother asked in that dry voice. "Does *she* miss him too?"

Taffy's motives seemed less clear to me, except that I think she's someone who's very eager to please and maybe convinced herself she saw something just to make my grandmother feel better. "Look, what does it matter?" I said. "You saw it, you believe in it, and I didn't. Probably we just look at things differently."

You could say the solution to this whole thing would just be to say to my grandmother: It's true, I do feel his spirit, I felt his eyes move. What harm would that do? But I just couldn't. I just stood there, immobilized. I felt my grandmother's and Taffy's eyes fixed on me. "I think I'll go to bed," I said.

My grandmother came close to me. "Do me a favor, dear. All right? Just for me. You don't have to believe in it. Will you just go up to the photo and say, 'Goodnight, Grandpa'?"

I hesitated a long time. Then I went over to the photo. "Goodnight, Grandpa," I said, feeling like a jackass.

Tears came to my grandmother's eyes. "Now was *that* so hard?" she said. "Think how happy you've made him just with those few words. Because all spirits have is words, words and feelings. Their bodies are gone."

"Maybe that's a nice feeling," Taffy put in. "Not to have a body."

My grandmother frowned. "No, I don't think it's nice. I think it's probably very painful." She turned to me. "Dear, walk Taffy home, will you? It's getting late."

"I can go by myself," Taffy said.

"No, Spencer would be happy to take you. It's just a short walk."

It was raining, so I went to get our big black umbrella and set off with Taffy holding my arm.

# 15

Taffy was silent most of the way, just holding my arm and walking close to my side. Maybe because I've been with Audrey so much, the physical closeness didn't bother me. I find Taffy attractive, but I didn't feel I'd lose control.

"Your grandmother must have loved your grandfather very much," she said.

"Yeah, I guess."

"I never talked to him that much," Taffy went on. "He always sort of scared me, the way he looked at you with those dark eyes. I like blue eyes better. They seem more friendly."

I didn't say anything.

"I guess really I came over to see you," Taffy said softly. "We haven't really seen each other since . . . that time."

"I think we better forget about that," I said. "It was a mistake on both our parts."

"No," Taffy said. "It wasn't! It was meant to be. It

155

means that we belong to each other now, that our bodies are one, not just our souls."

Jesus. "Taff, listen, if you belong to anyone, it's Linc, okay? And he's my friend. I don't want to interfere in his life."

Taffy's mouth was set in a firm line. "It's none of his business."

I tried to laugh. "Well, I think it kind of is, if you're his wife."

"I know you wouldn't do what we did with anyone you didn't love," Taffy said. "You're not that kind of person."

"Yes, I am," I said. "I'm doing it with someone right now, as a matter of fact."

Taffy stopped stock still. "Who?"

"Audrey, that girl I brought bowling."

"But she's divorced," Taffy said, "and she's older than you!" She looked horrified.

"So what?"

"You *can't* be doing it with her!"

"I am, okay? Almost every day."

Taffy's eyes looked frightened. "I don't believe you."

"Taffy, look, I didn't say I loved her in the way you mean. I just said we do it and I'm not ashamed of it. I'm *not* this wonderful, perfect person you imagine me to be. I'm not! That's your fantasy—like my grand-mother and the photo. You've got to stop thinking like that!"

"Okay," Taffy said very quietly. "I'll stop."

"I'm just a regular guy," I went on desperately. "Not everything I do is that consistent *or* that smart. I do lots of things I shouldn't. I shouldn't have laid a hand on you that night in the garden. That was bad, and I'm ashamed I did it."

"What if I get pregnant and it's your child?" Taffy said, looking up at me.

I froze. "What?"

"I'm just saying what if. . . . It *could* happen."

"How could it?"

Taffy laughed. "You know how, Spence."

"No, but I mean, don't you . . . don't you use anything?" I felt really sick.

"I have a diaphragm," Taffy said, "but it's at home. I don't go around wearing it all the time."

"Oh, God . . . Taffy, that wasn't right. You shouldn't have done that."

"Well, what's done is done," she said, almost the way my grandmother says it.

"You're, you're married to another guy, it's his kid, his responsibility. I'm going to college. I can't—"

"Look, it hasn't happened," Taffy said. "And I won't tell Linc, even if it does happen. I'll just raise it as though it's his. No one'll ever know except us."

"Oh, God."

"Why do you do it with that woman?" Taffy cried. "I don't understand."

"She's sexy, she turns me on." I felt so angry with Taffy I could hardly speak.

"More than me?"

"Yeah, more than you."

"Why? Because she's more experienced?" Taffy's voice was shaking.

"She's my girlfriend! You're my friend's wife. Don't you see the difference?"

"She doesn't even know you," Taffy said tearfully. "I've known you for ten years. . . . Didn't you even

157

enjoy it that time we did it? I asked you if you were happy afterward and you said yes."

"I said yes because I . . . I don't know." I felt so hopeless and awful I couldn't go on.

Taffy was breathing with difficulty. "Okay, well, I understand. You can do it with her if you want. You just need—an outlet. It's not love. You said it wasn't."

"Maybe it is," I said, defiantly. "I don't know."

"If it was, you'd know," Taffy said. "There's a difference between just doing it because of need and because of love."

"Yeah, well . . ." We were amost at her in-laws' house. "I have to get back home." I turned and walked off. Just at the end of the street I turned and looked back quickly over my shoulder, and there was Taffy, still standing in the exact same spot, gazing after me mournfully.

I felt so tense and upset I wanted to smash my fist into a wall. Damn girls! All they do is get you into some kind of trouble or other. Either they idealize you or they tear you down. If Taffy gets pregnant, I don't know what I'll do. It's not fair. It's just not playing fair.

Back at the house my grandmother was sitting in the living room sipping a cup of cocoa. The photo was lying down on the couch, half covered by the afghan. "Taffy is such a sweet girl," my grandmother said.

"She's crazy," I exploded.

"Spencer! Please!"

"Okay, she's a sweet girl, and Grandpa is really still alive and the photo is real and the moon is made of green cheese."

"I think you're behaving very badly," my grandmother said. "I don't see any excuse for it."

I started out the door.

"Where are you going?" my grandmother called, jumping up.

"To see my girlfriend."

"What girlfriend?"

"Audrey. I told you about her." I just wanted to get over there.

"It's eleven at night," my grandmother said. "You can't go over there now. What would her parents think?"

"Her father's gone and her mother stays with her boyfriend. She's by herself."

"I don't care," my grandmother said. "You are not doing that, Spencer, and I mean it. This is a small town, comparatively, and you could destroy her reputation if people see you going over there this late. I won't have it."

I pulled away. "She's twenty, she's divorced. . . . None of that matters."

"It matters very much," my grandmother said. "I won't have you treating women this way. They are not playthings to be used in such a cavalier manner. Look at poor little Taffy. Madly in love with you and you act like she's not even there. That won't do."

"Gran, I'm almost in college. I have my own life. Get off my case, will you?"

My grandmother turned white. "Go, then! Get out of this house! I don't know what's come over you, but you're not the same person."

"Right," I said. "I'm not." I slammed the door and jumped into the car.

Audrey was in bed, reading. Actually, she hadn't expected me to come over, and I hadn't been sure whether her mother would be there or not. "What's wrong?" she said, as I came careening in the door. It had started to pour again, and I was all soaked just in the brief dash from the car.

"My grandmother's going nuts," I said, not wanting to mention about Taffy. "I just can't take it."

"Poor sweetie." Audrey took me upstairs, helped me strip my clothes off, and wrapped me in her electric blanket to get warm. "I'll make you a rum toddy," she said. "You'll feel better."

Audrey sat on the bed while I sipped the drink and then slid in naked under the covers next to me, winding herself around me. As I reached for her, I felt as though I was sliding into some whirling cave. She let me go as fast as I wanted, and I could feel her teeth on my shoulder, hear her high-pitched, whimpering cries. In the middle of the night we made love again, more slowly. I fell asleep with her on top of me, like a big floppy rag doll, her hair brushing my ear.

The next day was Saturday. It was a day I was due at RGC. I only have about four more times to go, and I'm determined to see it through. Audrey asked if she could come with me. But now it doesn't seem to matter any more. I remember one thing I said in that essay I did in high school was that there shouldn't be too big a distance between your aspirations and what you can realistically achieve, and that if you keep blaming yourself for not being good enough, you'll use up all your energy that way and never get anything done. So maybe I did make some women happy this summer or will, once those sperm are actually used. I just wish it was as easy to make real women happy.

When I came out, Audrey was sitting outside in the shade, smoking. She had a straw hat on, a blue dress, and high-heeled white sandals. "Whatever happened to your cousin," I asked her, "the one who wasn't married but who wanted to get pregnant anyway?"

"She got some guy she knows to do it. She's not in love with him and he's not in love with her. Just—no strings. He won't have to see the kid or pay to raise it."

"What if he wants to?"

"No, he doesn't. . . . He's just doing her a favor. You know, it's funny. Mom says she knows the exact night she got pregnant with me. She says she could tell, right when it was happening. I don't believe in that, do you?"

I laughed and put my arm around her. "I never got pregnant, so I don't know."

Suddenly Audrey looked at me in that amused, detached way she has. "You're such a kid," she said, stroking my hair.

I looked away, hurt. Why does she say things like that after last night?

"I didn't mean it in a bad way," Audrey said. She blew smoke out languidly.

"Last night you didn't seem to think I was such a kid."

She kept stroking my hair. "Relax, sweetie. You're wonderful. You know that. You're a terrific lover."

"I am?"

"Sure . . . only I think maybe you should go home and tend to your grandmother."

"*Tend* to my grandmother?"

"She's suffered a terrible loss," Audrey said, "and she loves you. So pretend if it makes her happy. I do that with my mother. I know this guy won't marry her any more than he'll fly to the moon, but some nights

161

she just wants to sit there and dream about all the impossible things that'll never happen and I let her."

"I hate doing that," I said. "Pretending the photo is real. That's just craziness."

"It's something she needs now," Audrey said. "It'll pass."

I drove Audrey home and then went back to our house. As I pulled in the driveway, I started feeling guilty about the way I'd stormed out. I never used to fight with my grandmother. Maybe because my grandfather was always so irritating and she was the one who tried to make peace all the time. When I walked in, I called out, "Gran?"

"I'm in here," she called. She was in the kitchen, making Jello-O with peaches. "We haven't had Jell-O in such a long time, and since Omar couldn't bear peaches I got out of the habit. But I thought you and I could have a nice dinner together . . . *if* you're planning on being here."

"Yeah, I am." I knew this was the moment to apologize, but I just sood there, watching her stir the red gooey stuff around with a big spoon.

"I was worried about you, driving in the rain," she said tentatively.

"I drive slowly," I said. I squeezed her shoulder. "You don't have to worry."

My grandmother hunched over. "It's losing both of you at once, that's hard," she said. "First Omar, then you . . ."

"You're not losing me," I said. "I'm just going off to college."

"It was easier with the girls," she went on softly. "I don't know why. Maybe because there were more of

162

them. Maybe I was younger, more resilient. And you're my only grandson."

"I'm still your only grandson," I said wryly.

My grandmother pulled herself together. "I don't want to cling to you. You have our own life, you're going to go on way beyond all of us. I want you to! It's just—"

I took her hand. "Gran, listen, college is only two hundred miles away. I'll be back all the time, vacations. We'll talk on the phone. We can write letters."

Her face lit up. "Could we? I love writing letters. Remember that summer you were in Maine? I still have those wonderful letters you wrote, describing everything you saw. Each time one came, I'd read it aloud to Omar, then to the girls. Some of them I knew almost by heart."

I thought of how the whole point of the letters had been to communicate with my grandfather and how he'd never answered. My grandmother was putting the Jell-O away in the refrigerator. When she finished up, she said, "Tell me about your girlfriend. Is she nice?"

I didn't really feel like talking about Audrey. "Yeah, I like her a lot," I said. I was scared my grandmother could tell how much sex I'd been having just by looking at me. "But probably we won't see each other once I go away."

"Why is that?" my grandmother asked.

"Well, she's planning on going off to study," I said. "She wants to be a pilot. She was married before, so she's not that eager to settle down again right away."

"That's sensible," my grandmother said. "Though it must be hard for her."

"What's hard?"

"Giving you up for her career. She must feel terrible conflicts about that."

"I—I don't know," I said.

My grandmother's eyes were fixed on me with that anxious, concerned expression. "But you love each other?" she said. "It isn't just . . . a physical relationship?"

What could I say to that? "Basically," I said. "I mean, it's physical too, but—"

My grandmother was staring out the window. "It would bother me if I felt you were taking advantage of her," she said. "That's all I meant to say."

"No," I said. "I'm not."

"Women may not always show it," she went on, "but they seem to care more strongly for men when there's a . . . physical aspect to the relationship."

I felt extremely uncomfortable talking about this with her. "I think that was more in the old days, Gran."

"Things never really change," my grandmother said. "Just superficially. The basics never change."

# 16

Over dinner we planned the day we would go out to sprinkle my grandfather's ashes over Lake Paloma. "Let's just have it the two of us," she said. "I don't want to make a whole to-do. Omar wouldn't have wanted that."

I found a few poems that I thought might be good to read and showed them to my grandmother. "You know what I'll do," she said. "I'll read them to him and see which one he seems to respond to most."

It seemed weirdly contradictory to me for my grandmother to be planning to dispose of my grandfather's ashes, the remains of his physical body, yet still carrying on about the photo. I was hoping that the ceremony on the lake might put an end to that. I know she feels ashamed to do it too much in front of me, though the two of them still watch *The Yellow Ribbon* at night. But a few times I've come into the house quietly and heard her talking to the photo. In the late afternoon she moves him up on the landing so he can

165

"see" out into the garden. "It's such a lovely day today, dear," I hear her say. "The light is so incredible. And I thought how unfair it is to have you downstairs all the time, in that dark living room." She told him about me being about to go off to college. I even heard her tell him about Audrey. "I haven't met her yet, but Spencer has such good taste in girls. She sounds like a lovely young woman, more mature than some of those girls he used to see in high school. She has a career all picked out for herself—well, you know how it is these days."

I try as hard as I can to be more tolerant about what my grandmother is doing. Really, what she's doing is acting the same way to the photo of my grandfather as she did to my real grandfather while he was alive: tending to his needs, making sure he's comfortable, conversing with him even when he doesn't say anything in return. I used to think all that was kind of a burden for her, but maybe she misses it.

I was over at Carnie's one evening and she said she was concerned about it, too. "I wonder what would happen if I took the photo away," I said.

"What do you mean?"

"Just hid it or threw it out."

Mercer was there, sitting in his chair, reading. I couldn't see him from behind the newspaper, but he said, "No, don't do that, Spence."

"Why not? Maybe a clean break is what she needs. Cold turkey."

He tilted his paper down a little. "She's not hurting anyone, is she? What's wrong with it?"

"Sweetie, if it were someone in your family you'd feel differently," Carnie said.

"If my father kicked the bucket, my mother'd shed

166

one quick tear and wouldn't give him another thought," Mercer said.

"I wish she'd get interested in other things," Carnie went on. "It's such a pity you'll be leaving for college so soon, Spence."

At that Mercer put his paper down altogether. "It is not! It's a damn good thing. Spencer has his own life . . . and Margaret had better find one for herself."

Carnie sighed. "Men are so . . . sensible!" she said wryly.

"I'm not going all that far away," I said. "It's not the end of the world."

"Listen, kid," Mercer said. "You just go, you hear me? You've grown up with all these women hovering around you, telling you what to do, taking care of you. Now's the time to put all that behind you, find your own way."

"Yeah, well, that's what I intend to do," I said.

"That's a terrible distortion," Carnie said, looking angry. "We haven't hovered. Have we, Spence? We love him—that's not a crime."

Mercer winked at me. "How's your girlfriend?"

I turned red. "Oh, she's good."

"I'll bet she is. . . . I saw the two of you together one day. She's miles ahead of most of the women around this town."

Carnie looked at him, her head tilted to one side. "I didn't know you noticed," she said.

He smiled. "You never stop noticing," he said.

"Is she the one who's older than you are?" Carnie asked me.

I felt embarrassed. "Just two years. It's more that she's been divorced. She married real young, right out of high school."

"Perfect," Mercer said. "My first girlfriend was eight years older. That's the way, they know the ropes, they know you're going to move on eventually."

"I think that's awfully cynical," Carnie said. "What's to stop Spencer from marrying her just because she's two years older?"

"He's a baby," Mercer said, smiling at me. "Give him a chance. Let him have some fun out of life."

Even though their bantering was affectionate, I felt a little awkward. "I'm certainly not going to get married," I said. "Not for a while. I have some friends from school who did that, and they seem pretty miserable."

"Taffy and Linc?" Carnie said. "Oh, that poor little girl. Talk about babies!"

I held my tongue. Taffy isn't quite the baby everyone takes her for. "The way that girl used to look at you was pathetic," Carnie said. "Blind love. She would've done *anything* for you!"

Mercer stood up and went over to Carnie. He began rubbing her neck. "Why, honey, I thought that was the way all women felt about their men, isn't it? You look at me that way."

She reached her hand up and stroked one of his. "Well, maybe you deserve it some of the time."

"I guess I do." Mercer smiled down at her.

The day we'd planned to sprinkle my grandfather's ashes in the lake was overcast. The paper predicted a thunderstorm late in the day so my grandmother decided we should go right after lunch. We drove down to the edge of the lake where they rent rowboats and canoes. I picked a solid-looking rowboat. My grandmother had the ashes in a little jar. She was holding onto it tightly, like it might jump out of her hands. "I asked Omar this morning if this was still what he wanted," she said as she settled into the back of the boat. "He said it was."

I started rowing. We'd decided we would row about halfway across so the ashes wouldn't just be swept back to shore. I like rowing, the steady rhythm of the oars dipping into the water. There weren't many boats out, I guess because of the grayness of the day. "Are you still going to—you know—do all that stuff with the photo after this?" I asked.

My grandmother was wearing a yellow dress with little flowers on it. She had a little straw hat on with a ribbon around it. "It's not up to me," she said. "It's not that simple, Spence. I've told Omar time and time again—if he wants to return totally to the world of the spirits, I'll understand. After all—think how hard it must be for him this way. But it was always so hard for him, making new friends. And it probably isn't that different for him where he is now."

I had a strange feeling being with my grandmother in the middle of the lake, her holding the jar with my grandfather's ashes, everything so still and heavy around us. I almost imagined him watching this, exclaiming the way he used to so often, "What *is* all this tomfoolery?" "I think you're right," I said. "I think he ought to just go. . . . After all, we're alive and he's not."

"It may not be as different as we assume," my grandmother said. "They still have thoughts and feelings even when all that's left of their bodies is a bunch of ashes." She smiled shyly. "That's why I wore this dress. It was Omar's favorite. He may not see me exactly, but he knows I'm in this dress." She patted the jar, running her finger along the top of it.

I figured we were far enough out now. I stopped the boat and put the oars up. Then I got out the book of poems. "Should I read it or you?" I asked my grandmother.

"You read it," she said. "You read so beautifully."

I read the poem. It was by A. E. Housman. We had to learn it for school, and it was the only poem I can remember my grandfather liking. It's called "When I Watch the Living Meet."

When I watch the living meet,
   And the moving pageant file
Warm and breathing through the street
   Where I lodge a little while,

If the heats of hate and lust
   In the house of flesh are strong,
Let me mind the house of dust
   Where my sojourn shall be long.

In the nation that is not
   Nothing stands that stood before;
There revenges are forgot,
   And the hater hates no more.

Lovers lying two and two
   Ask not whom they sleep beside,
And the bridegroom all night through
   Never turns him to the bride.

Reading it aloud to my grandmother, I was more aware of the lines about lust and "in the house of flesh" and the part at the end about lovers lying side by side. But she didn't seem to notice that. She just sat there dreamily, and finally said, "That's lovely, Spence . . . 'the house of dust.' That's so pretty. And it's true—all of our petty little hates and envies. What's the point, really? It's all over so fast."

"Sure," I said.

Then my grandmother opened the jar and scattered the ashes into the lake. They held for a moment on the surface and then vanished into the water. We both sat watching them. "Well," my grandmother said, looking sad. "That's that. Let's just sit here a minute. I don't think it'll rain for a while yet. Let's each try and think of times we had with Omar when we felt really close to him."

I tried, but I have to admit none came to me. I thought of all those times I would bring up a conversational topic and he'd cock his head to one side or make some disparaging remark. About the only positive thing I could remember was once, when someone bought me a little boat for Christmas and it turned out to be the kind you had to glue together. I was only seven or eight and couldn't figure out the complicated instructions that came with it. Omar sat down and studied the instructions for a long time. "We're going to do this, boy," he said. "We'll figure it out, don't you worry. We won't let this lick us." He spread all the pieces out on the table and gradually we managed to get it put together. It never looked too much like the boat they showed on the cover of the box, but at least it was a boat.

After a while I started rowing back.

"I didn't always feel I got through to him," my grandmother said. "I admit that. Sometimes it was like talking to a wall. He'd sit there and stare, like I wasn't there!"

"Yeah, I know," I said.

"It was the war," she said. "He had some kind of—what do they call it. He was mentally affected by it, the noise, seeing people killed. He told me once he dreamed about that once a week every night of his life."

I hadn't known about that. "I thought he wasn't in combat," I said.

"They sent him back after a month," my grandmother said. "He started cracking up. He never told you because he wanted you to admire him. To tell the truth, I think he was scared out of his wits, and I don't blame him. He wasn't a military man at heart. And he never would have done it if his father hadn't insisted. That's why he never forced you into anything. He wanted you to feel free to go your own way, lead your own life."

I started wondering what it'll be like if I have a son. It's true I wouldn't want to force him to do anything special, but I sure hope I can talk to him. My father, in the photos of him I've seen, looks like someone I could've talked to. I get the feeling he was sort of the opposite of my grandfather—a low-key, very friendly guy, not that ambitious. He loved baseball, camping out. He used to make dollhouse furniture for my sisters in the basement. From what my sisters say, my mother was more outgoing, loved to dance, wasn't very good at sports. I imagine her like a cross between Lizzie and Carnie, laughing a lot, getting a kick out of life. Even though I was supposed to be sitting there, thinking of my grandfather, I realized I was thinking about my parents. How can you miss someone you've never even known? I'm not sure, but I do.

My grandmother carried the jar back to the house,

rinsed it out and put it with all the other jars she keeps for leftovers. I was surprised. I'd thought she would regard it as a special jar since it'd held my grandfather's ashes. "It's just a jar," she said, seeming surprised when I asked her. "We mustn't make more of things than they really are. A jar is a jar."

But despite that, an hour later, I heard her up on the landing telling the photo of my grandfather all about the ceremony and how beautifully I'd read the poem and how I'd rowed clear to the middle of the lake. "It was wonderful," she said. "I wish so much you had been there, dear."

# 17

I'm getting ready for college now, packing my things. I've started being conscious that everything I do is for the last time. The last time I went to the clinic, I stopped in to see Dr. Galardo on my way out. The secretary said he wanted me to.

"Well," he said. "I want to thank you for taking part in this experiment with us, Spencer. We really appreciate it, and—time will tell whether it's been a good idea or not."

"What do you mean?" I asked. "Why shouldn't it be a good idea?"

Dr. Galardo is a small man with a moustache. He has a way of squinching up his eyes when he talks as though he was having trouble seeing. "We don't know the long-range effects," he said, "on the families, how the fathers will take to it. After all, with adoption both parents know that it isn't their child. In this situation, it is, technically, the mother's child, but not the father's. That could cause problems."

"But the mothers'll be happy," I said. "Right?"

"Right. Through us, through the efforts of all of us, they'll have the unique experience of birth. That's no small thing."

"Do you have kids?" I asked him.

He held up three fingers. "Two boys and a girl. And you want to know something interesting? They all look exactly like their mother. So, who's to tell? I always tell the fathers who come in here that it's the input they have in their children after birth that counts, not just the genetic setup. That's just the raw material. You provided that."

Now that it's over I feel proud I did take part in doing this, though I don't know if I'd want to do it again. I didn't tell Dr. Galardo that I had a girlfriend for part of the summer. The fact is, he never told me I couldn't. All he said was that I had to take my part seriously and not forget to show up. I never forgot to show up.

"You're off to college now?" he asked, getting up.

"Yeah, I leave in a week."

"Good for you. And thanks again."

As I walked out, I looked behind the building.

Someone tapped me on the shoulder. I turned and saw a young woman with a round pretty face and dark hair. "Could you tell me where the clinic is?" she asked.

"Which one?"

"I think it's called—" She took a piece of paper. "The Michigan Repository of Germinal Choice."

"It's right over there," I said. Then, for some reason. I added, "I just came from there."

She looked surprised. "I thought it was just for

women. I thought it was for helping women who had trouble getting pregnant."

"I'm a donor," I explained. "I mean, I was, for the summer."

"Oh." She looked at me a long time. "You mean, you're one of the men who, you're one of the ones who . . ."

I straightened up, trying to look like someone she'd be proud to have as the father of her child. "Yeah," I said.

"But you're so young!" she said.

I turned red. "I'm eighteen."

"Goodness . . . I just never thought . . . I always imagined the donors as wise old men who had accomplished all kinds of remarkable things."

"Wise old men might not have such active sperm," I said. "Anyway, maybe I will accomplish remarkable things. I haven't had that much time yet."

She smiled. "Well, good luck. I hope you do." She reached out and shook my hand."

"Good luck to you, too," I said. I watched her walk off to the clinic. I don't know why, but it made me feel good that I'd finally, before I went away, met a real woman who might some day bear my child. She wasn't especially beautiful or anything, but she was real.

Rob was leaving for college a week before I was. I'd promised to drop over to his house to help him load his car. Actually, by the time I got there, it was mostly loaded, so we just sat outside and waited for his father to get back home to say goodbye. Rob kept looking at his watch. "This is so typical," he said. "He made such a big deal out of how I shouldn't leave without saying goodbye to him, and now he's at his girlfriend's and he's probably forgotten all about it."

Rob had strapped his bike on top of his car. He looked up at it, as though hoping it was really secure. "They let you have bikes in your rooms," he said. "I checked on that."

"How about girls?" I asked.

"What about them?"

"Can you have girls in your rooms? Some land-ladies don't allow it."

He shrugged. "I didn't ask about that."

That's typical of Rob, not even asking about girls, but remembering to ask about his bicycle. I remember when he got it. We were in tenth grade. It has six speeds and can go like the wind. "I'm going to be in a coed dorm," I said, "so I guess that won't be any problem."

"What won't?" Rob asked, in his abstracted way.

"Girls!" I yelled.

Rob looked glum. "Like you said, it'll happen eventually. The main thing is not to rush it, not to think about it too much." He looked at me. "Did you ever make it with that girl you were seeing over the summer? The one who wanted to be a pilot?"

"Yeah," I said, adding, "quite a few times, actually?"

"I figured you had," Rob said gloomily. "You acted different."

I was surprised at that. "How did I act different?"

"Oh, sometimes you'd just sit there with a kind of self-satisfied smile, like you were remembering some-thing terrific. It really got me pissed."

I laughed. "It *was* terrific . . . most of the time."

"Don't tell me about it. I don't want to get all crazy while I'm driving."

I put my hand on his shoulder. "It'll happen to you."

"Yeah, I know," Rob said. He looked down the road. "Was she really—did she seem to enjoy it?"

"I thought you didn't want to talk about it."

"I don't want to hear all kinds of lurid details . . . I just wondered if girls really enjoyed it. Of course, you said she was a nymphomaniac. I guess they're different."

"That was stupid," I said, feeling ashamed as I remembered. "She's not. I just said that because we had a fight once."

"Maybe I'll meet a nymphomaniac at Wayne State," Rob said.

"That's just a word people use. Just find someone who likes you, who's basically relaxed. It's not that complicated."

Rob looked angry. "Yes, it is!" he said. "Everything's complicated. Everything in the whole goddamn world is complicated."

At that moment his father's car pulled up and he jumped out. "I haven't kept you waiting, have I?" he said. "I got a little detained with Suzanne." He grinned.

"Yeah, you did," Rob said. "I was supposed to set out an hour ago."

"It's two o'clock," his father said. "Relax! . . . Well, what can I say? Have fun, study hard, write occasionally . . ."

"Okay," Rob said. He still looked annoyed. "I will."

His father turned to me. "When're you setting off, Spencer?"

"Next week," I said.

"I know you two are going to miss each other," he said. "Girls may come and go, but a good friend is worth his weight in gold. You remember that."

Rob rolled his eyes.

"Have you bid your mother farewell?" his father asked.

"Yup . . . I did that this morning."

His father looked uncomfortable. "How *is* she? . . . Is she taking it all right?"

"Yeah, she's fine," Rob said impatiently. "Hey, Dad, I've got to go, okay? I'm late as it is."

His father clapped him on the back. "Have a great year? You too, Spence. I'll keep the home fires burning."

"Asshole," Rob said under his breath as we drove off. Rob had said he wanted to say goodbye to Linc quickly and drive me home. I still hadn't told Rob about Taffy. I don't know why that one thing seemed so hard to talk about or even think about, but it did. I was praying Taffy might not be around. She didn't seem to be. Or at least when we rang the front doorbell, Linc came to the door. He walked out on the lawn with us. "Taffy's out shopping," he said. "She says to tell you goodbye."

Rob's face softened. "Tell her I'm sorry I didn't have a chance to see her."

Linc was looking off in the distance. "Maybe we'll drive up and visit you," he said.

"That'd be good," Rob said.

"Boy, I envy you two," Linc said. "I'd sell my soul

ten times over to be setting off now, unencumbered . . ."

"Listen," Rob said. "You have a good family, a kid, a beautiful wife . . . I could envy *you* if I felt like it. Why don't you appreciate what you've got?"

Linc smiled weakly. "Yeah, right . . . good advice." He glanced at me.

Even that glance made me uncomfortable. "How, uh, *is* Taffy?" I asked. "Has she been okay?"

He shrugged. "Well, she's kind of . . . I don't know. I guess I don't understand her. I thought if we got married, that'd be all she'd want or need to make her happy, but I was evidently wrong."

"It'll be okay," I said, glad I wasn't Linc. I knew how he must feel and felt sorry for him.

Rob drove me back to my house. "People never appreciate what they have," he said.

I knew he didn't really understand the situation with Linc and Taffy, but all I said was, "Sure." I told him I'd write, and we agreed we'd get together sometime before Christmas.

"Tell your grandmother so long," he said, as he drove off.

It's going to be hard with girls at college, after Audrey. With her I never felt I had to do much convincing or explaining. I wish she could come up there and be with me. When I saw her that night I brought that up. "I mean, as long as you just have a job in a travel agency, you could do that in Ann Arbor," I said.

Her face froze. "That's just temporary," she said. "I'm trying to save up for flying school."

We were in her room with the door closed. We'd made love more quietly than usual because her mother was home. Her mother knows all about us, but I never feel that comfortable with her there, even though she was downstairs in the living room, watching TV. "Yeah, well, all I meant was you could get a temporary job there."

"And just wait around for you to get back from classes and fuck me?"

"No." Obviously I wasn't explaining it right. "I just think I'm going to miss you."

She looked away, a grim expression on her face. "You'll miss me for one second and then you'll be into a whole new life, your studies, girls. . . . By Christmas you won't even remember who I am!"

"I will!" I insisted. "I'm not like that! I'm not that kind of person."

Audrey had a wary expression. She was lying flat on her back, with the sheet drawn up to her neck. Usually she just lies around naked without seeming self-conscious about it at all. "There's something I should tell you," she said.

"What?"

But she just looked at me. "I don't think I can."

"Why not?"

"It's about us."

"So, tell me!"

"I'll write you about it once you get to college. Is that okay?"

"Sure . . . I just don't understand why you can't tell me now."

"You might be angry. You're only a teenager and—"

I grabbed her shoulder. "I hate it when you do that! Five minutes ago you said I was wonderful, that I satisfied you in every way."

Audrey sat up and smiled. "No, you do, you do."

"You act like this was just some summer romance. It doesn't have to be. We could go on seeing each other. We could get married even, eventually."

"No, we couldn't," Audrey said. "That's crazy."

"Why not? I don't mean now . . . like in ten years."

She laughed. "Ten *years*? You can wait that long?"

"Well, I'll be studying a lot. I mean we could both see other people, but—"

"Ten years." Audrey looked like she was going to cry. "In ten years I'll probably still be working away at some dead-end job, dreaming crazy dreams about some future that'll never come to pass."

"It'll come to pass," I said, taken aback by the bitterness in her voice. "Why shouldn't it? If you believe in yourself—"

"It takes so much more than that," Audrey said. "Especially if you're a woman. So much work, luck, determination. I don't know if I have it."

"Sure you do," I said.

"I talk a good line," she said, "but I'm afraid I'm just going to end up like my mother, raising some kid in a hick town, hoping for some 'better life,' quote unquote."

I don't know what it was, hearing her bitter, sad voice, knowing we wouldn't be seeing each other for a while, but I said, "If you want, we could get married right now."

"How would that solve anything I've been talking about?" Audrey snapped.

"You'd have someone to believe in you, even if you don't believe in yourself."

She sighed. "You really think I'm going to be pilot one day?"

"Sure."

"On the basis of what? This?" She pointed to our naked bodies.

"No, just because I know you're a smart, good person."

Audrey snuggled up and pressed close against me. "Spence," she murmured. "I'm ging to miss you so damn much."

I had an idea. "Why don't you drive with me up to school? You could stay over and take the bus back on Sunday." I felt excited at the idea. I hate long drives by myself.

"You're leaving Saturday?"

"I'll come by for you around noon, how's that?" I kissed her neck and then slid my mouth down to her breasts. She smelled of lemons, like Christmas cookies.

"That's wonderful," Audrey said. "Keep right on . . . yes, okay, why not?"

I had thought I'd feel sad, leaving Audrey that night, knowing it would be the last time I'd see her, but instead I felt exicted and good, thinking about our trip together. I feel bad when she gets into moods like the one she was in tonight. I remember how she told me the first night we spent together that she was a moody person, but I didn't know exactly what she meant. It's funny because I think I'm a fairly good-natured person. I don't mean I'm on an even keel every second, but basically I tackle the problems at hand the best I can and don't let it bother me if I can't. But the people I'm drawn to, of both sexes, like Rob and Audrey, are usually kind of emotional, intense people. Maybe it's that a part of me almost envies them, even though I can see basically it doesn't do them any good. But at least they just let it all hang out.

I started thinking about the future, about Audrey and me like one of those couples in *People* magazine. I'd be a doctor in some big city, and she'd be flying with some commercial airline. Possibly we'd have kids, but we could hire someone to look after them. We could just have one or two so it wouldn't be too much of a bother. I guess I hope they'll be boys just because it seems like all my life I've had nothing but women around me. It might be nice to have sons to talk to about all the things I never had a chance to talk to my father about. I think I'd be a good father, I really do.

When I walk into my grandmother's house after having been with Audrey, I feel like my body is coated with some radioactive material that glows all around me. She just looks up and says, "Hi, dear. Did you have a nice evening?" And no matter what I say, I have the feeling she knows how many times we made love and how good it was and what I felt. It's crazy, but I think maybe it's true.

"Yeah, it was good." I think I won't tell my grandmother Audrey is driving to Ann Arbor with me. She thinks it's a summer romance and might get worried if she thought it wasn't. "How was *The Yellow Ribbon*?" I said.

My grandother smiled. "Oh, I've given up on that. Such a silly program! And, you know, I looked over at Omar in the middle of it and he wasn't paying any more attention to it than *I* was! He looked as bored as bored can be. And then I realized why *should* he want to keep on watching it now? He watched it enough while he was alive."

"True," I said. My new policy with my grandmother and the photo is not to get into arguing with her or trying to change her mind. I just answer the immediate question.

"But you know," my grandmother went on, "I looked at him tonight, and he looked so thin and pale to me. I just hope he's getting enough to eat up there."

"Sure he is," I said indulgently. I felt so good, it wasn't bothering me as much as usual.

"For all we know, spirits don't need actual nourishment," my grandmother went on. "They may just exist on air or who knows what. But the trouble with Omar is he's so forgetful about things like that. If I went away for a day to visit my mother and I'd come back toward evening and ask him what he'd had for lunch, he'd say, 'Oh, I forgot.'"

I was starting to jiggle my leg, which is something I do when I'm nervous. "I think I'll get something to drink," I said.

"Oh, let me fix you some cocoa," my grandmother said. "Taffy was over here earlier, and she looked so thin and peaked, I fixed her some cocoa with real milk."

I froze. "What'd she come over for?"

"Just to see me, I think." My grandmother got the milk out of the refrigerator. "What a pathetic, sad little creature she is! And yet isn't it funny? Here you and all of my own girls treat me like some loony for trying to communicate with Omar, and Taffy, who isn't even my own blood, understands it perfectly. How do you explain that?"

"I don't," I said.

My grandmother poured the hot milk into a mug and stirred it around thoughtfully. "I asked her about the way Omar looked, and she said yes, he did look thinner and more pale to her. She knew right away what I meant! I think she has a spiritual streak to her, which is unusual in a young person. . . . Oh, and she adores you, Spence! It's sad, in a way, but I think deep down she made a mistake marrying Lincoln, though he's a fine young man. I somehow don't think he has her undivided love and attention.

"Well, but she did marry him," I said. "So shouldn't she concentrate on that?"

My grandmother looked taken aback. "Of course, dear. Don't misunderstand me. I just said I think with a girl like Taffy who's so gentle and sweet and, well, otherworldly almost, she should have waited for someone who would have appreciated her for those qualities. As you would have."

The cocoa was great, but I was getting all worked up, which I had promised myself I wouldn't. "Gran, I don't think I'm even halfway ready to get married. She'd have been *worse* off with me, a lot worse."

My grandmother gave me a long grave stare.

"You're a sensible boy, Spencer. Of course you wouldn't marry a girl straight out of high school like that. I give you credit for more sense than *that!*"

"I couldn't be interested in Taffy," I said. "It wouldn't be right."

My grandmother had her head to one side, the way she does when she's displeased. "Of course you couldn't! She's another man's wife! I know what high moral standards you have. I'm not accusing you of anything."

I can never tell with my grandmother how much she

knows or intuits and how much I just think she does. For one horrible second I imagined that Taffy had told her about that night in the garden. I must have looked upset, because my grandmother patted my arm. "We can't always be responsible for who loves us," she said. "What Taffy feels for you is her own affair. And perhaps it's just something she needs, some fantasy that makes her real life more bearable."

Like you and the photo, I thought. Suddenly, uncontrollably, I yawned. "Sorry," I said.

"Well, you've been working hard," my grandmother said. "Why don't you go up to bed? I'll clear up these dishes."

How did she mean that? Working hard? In bed with Audrey? My grandmother has this peculiar dry way of expressing herself which I never can interpret exactly. I wasn't sure if she meant the opposite, that I hadn't been working much at all, or what. But I decided to let it lie.

But in bed I replayed the whole evening in my head. I hate to say this, but deep down I'm afraid maybe I'll never in my life have as good sex with anyone as I've had with Audrey. You could say what do I know since she's the first person, and maybe it's always fantastic with the first person you do it with. But it's that, no matter how we sometimes fight or don't get along in other ways, when we're in bed together, I feel like she loves my whole body, even parts of it I've always felt self-conscious about. Like, I have these warts on my back, maybe half a dozen of them. I know I could have them removed surgically and maybe I will someday. Once by chance Emmy Lou put her hand on one and drew it back like she'd touched a slug. But Audrey will run her hands over them and not seem to mind at all. It's not that I've ever felt like I have an unattractive body, but my grandparents were really pretty untight about even partial nudity. If I even answered the phone in my bathrobe, my grandmother looked disapproving. Or, if I ran out of jockey shorts, she would buy me some new ones, but just say, "Spencer, I took the opportunity of replenishing your wardrobe today," as though referring directly to underpants was a dirty thing!

I've always known I was good at sports and pretty smart, but I never really knew, till this summer, that maybe I had other talents, too, and that maybe they were just as important as the part of me that got me a scholarship into college. It's okay being a donor, but someday I want to make some real woman happy, just like my father did with my mother.

# 18

"Surprise!"

I'd just walked in the door, from having taken the car to be checked over for my trip, when everyone, my whole family, came jumping out at me: all my sisters, their husbands, my grandmother. "Hey, what's going on?" I said.

"It's a farewell party," Lizzy said, kissing me. "We're all going to miss you so much."

I know if my grandfather were alive, there wouldn't have been any party because he hated noise and fuss and people getting drunk, so I hadn't expected this. I moved into the living room while all my sisters gathered around, chattering away, shoving presents at me. Mercer had even brought six bottles of pink champagne.

"This is what Omar and I drank on our honeymoon," my grandmother said and blushed. "He had it sent to our room."

I saw that the photo was still "sitting" in the chair,

with the sweater over its shoulders. Looking back, I took the glass Mercer handed me. "So, are you all set, kid?" he said. "How am I going to run the business without you?"

I couldn't help remembering the day the fixture broke. "I guess you'll have a hard time," I said.

"Kidding aside," he went on. "You've done a great job. It's been a big help to me."

"Spencer was always good with his hands," June said. "Silas was so impressed when you helped him repair his violin bow that day. He said you had the hands of an artist."

"Oh-ho," Jake, Willa's husband, said. "*That* sounds incriminatory."

Willa looked at him reprovingly. "It's true . . . Spencer intends to be a surgeon, and you need good steady hands for that."

"God, I wish you hadn't bought champagne," Lizzie said to Mercer. "I'm going to get silly drunk and say dopey things . . . or do dopey things, which is worse."

"As long as you do them with me, that's okay," Dan said. He was my coach in high school and he and Lizzie've been living together since I was in ninth grade. "Hey, listen, folks, we have an announcement to make."

Lizzie downed her glass of champagne. "We're getting married!"

"Congratulations," I said, kissing her on the lips. I was a little high myself. Lizzie is a very kissable person, even if she is my sister.

"When's it going to be?" Carnie asked.

"We haven't picked the day yet. . . . Will you

192

drive in from college, Spence?" Lizzie looked at me, bright-eyed and pretty.

"Sure, I will." I was just a kid when my other sisters got married, and June eloped with Silas because she knew my grandfather would disapprove.

"Will you have a long white dress?" June asked, looking excited.

"The works!" Lizzie crowed. "Remember how Grandpa used to say, if you're not a virgin, you can't have a church wedding. I used to say to him, 'Grandpa, if only virgins could marry in church weddings, the church'd have to close down shop immediately.'"

"He didn't mean it that way," my grandmother put in gently. "He just was afraid . . ."

"Of what?" Lizzie said. "Oh, I know, living in sin. What was that phrase? If you get the cow free, you won't go to the store for milk? Was that it?" She looked around the room. "So, here you all got free cows, and you married us anyway."

Jake boomed out with his hearty laugh. "Free cows! We did better than that. Prize heifers more likely."

Lizzie walked over to the photo. "Grandpa, will you forgive me? I'm a virgin at heart. And Dan is a sweet wonderful guy and we're going to be as happy as can be."

I'd thought my grandmother would be upset at that, but she just said, "He approves, Lizzie. That was just his manner, that way of acting gruff. And that's why he's come back to be with us at a time like this, to show that he approves."

There was a moment of total silence.

Then Willa said, "Gran, we feel like you should

stop going on about the photo. We really do. It's not good for you. It's living in the past."

My grandmother looked anxious. "Spencer doesn't think that, do you, dear? He understands."

Everyone looked at me. I wondered why my grandmother would say that. I thought I had been disapproving. "I think Gran should do what makes her happy," I said uncomfortably.

"Me, too," Carnie put in. "Willa, you go to church. Well, to some of us that's just as much an effort of the imagination."

Willa's face was turning red. "It's not the same thing at all," she said stiffly.

"The old guy isn't harming anyone," Jake said. He always called my grandfather "the old guy," even when he was alive.

"He's free to go," my grandmother said. "I've told him that many times. Of course I'll miss you, I've said, but if it makes you happier to go, that's fine. Go!"

"Are you all packed and ready, hon?" Carnie asked me.

"I'm driving up alone," I told her. "I want to kind of gather my thoughts. Get in gear for being a student again."

June had been sitting quietly, just sipping from her glass, like she always does. "I think that's sensible, Spence. I always like doing that, mentally recharging by being alone. It's a new life for you, after all."

"A new life," Mercer said, refilling everyone's glass. "Margaret, drink up. I got this especially for you."

My grandmother isn't much of a drinker either, but she allowed him to fill her glass. "I'm torn between

194

happiness and sadness," she mused. "I'll miss Spencer something terrible. What can I do?"

Lizzie let out a whoop. "Oh, Lord, Gran, leave the poor guy be. Here he survived eighteen years with five females clucking and feathering around him. He deserves a break, some freedom."

"Oh, I know," my grandmother said, still looking sad.

"Will you write us?" Carnie asked. "You can just write one letter and Mercer can Xerox it. That'll save time."

"Sure, I'll write," I said, trying not to hiccup again. "Every week."

"Spencer is such a wonderful writer." My grandmother perked up suddenly. "Omar and I used to wait breathlessly for the mail." She glanced at the photo. "Now look how pleased he looks! For the first time in weeks! He's been looking so peaked and drawn and worried, and now, suddenly, just while we were sitting here, he perked up and now he's downright serene."

We all looked at the photo.

"He was a handsome man," Lizzie remarked.

"Oh, yes," my grandmother said. "When we got engaged, his mother said to me, 'My dear, you beat out half the women for four counties around. He was known as the handsomest man in the marines.'"

Maybe it was being drunk, the way your mood can slide from way up to way down, but I suddenly, for the first time, felt aware that my parents were dead, my grandfather was dead, and that someday I wouldn't exist either, that all of us, all my sisters, even, would just be gone. It was a cold, empty feeling which seemed to freeze everything in the room.

"Spencer looks tired," Carnie said. "We should let

him have his sleep. He has to make an early start tomorrow."

I was grateful to her for saying that. I felt like I was spiraling down and down and knew I'd feel even worse if I didn't hit the sack soon. All my sisters kissed and hugged me goodbye. Their husbands clapped me on the back and said they hoped I'd have a good trip.

I thanked all of them for the party and went to bed.

# 19

"Well, where is she?"

I had pulled up in front of Audrey's house and found her not in. Her mother, sitting in the kitchen, said she'd gone away for the weekend. "Didn't she leave a note or anything?" I felt so upset I could hardly speak.

"She said she'd write you at college," her mother said. She had a tight, frightened expression.

"She was supposed to drive up with me," I said, confused. "What happened?"

"I believe something came up." She looked away.

"What? Why didn't she call me?"

"I don't know," her mother said. "I'm sorry. I just don't know."

I stood there, feeling so angry I wanted to smash something. To tell me she'd come with me, then back out, no call, no note! It wasn't Audrey's mother's fault, and she looked so scared and nervous, I didn't want to take it out on her. I just slammed out of the house, got into the car, and started the engine up

197

again. I didn't start driving right away. I was afraid I'd start speeding or do crazy things. I sat with my head bent over the steering wheel, numb. All I wanted was to get the trip over with as soon as I could. If I'd been going with Audrey, I would've taken the trip slowly. We could have stopped off for lunch. I'd even checked our Road Atlas for good places to eat. I was wearing a tie, for God's sake!

I tried to calm myself down, saying that maybe something important had come up which for some reason she couldn't tell me about. But what? And why not tell me just that? Unless it came up really suddenly, like in the middle of the night. For the first hour of the trip I kept seeing and hearing Audrey in my mind: her face, her body, her voice. Little snatches of dialogue between us would flash through my head, some good memories of great times we'd had together, other painful ones. But by the time I stopped for gas I felt better. Driving always relaxes me. I'm a good driver; I go fast, but I'm careful. It was a big highway so I decided to try and get some good music on the radio once I was back on the road.

"Could you check the tires?" I asked the gas station attendant. "That back one especially."

While he was checking the tires, I went and got a Coke from the vending machine. It was a beautiful day, hot, with a cool breeze. For the first time I felt excited about college, meeting new friends, maybe having a few excellent teachers. A new life, like June had said. I stretched, crumpled the can up and tossed it in the trash can.

Since I was alone, I decided not to make a big production out of lunch. I pulled up near a diner, went in, ordered a sandwich and salad, and ate it, studying the map and trying to decide which route to take once I came to the end of the thruway. Now that I thought of it, maybe it hadn't been such a smart idea to suggest to Audrey she come along with me. The important thing was to focus on college, on what lay ahead, not on the past. Maybe she'd sensed that and hadn't shown up because she didn't want to hinder me. It's sure hard to figure out the motivations of women sometimes.

I used the rest room, thought of calling my grandmother, but figured it was too soon, and got back on the road. Not counting stops for lunch and a break I took at three just to stretch and relieve the monotony, I made the trip in four hours. As I was nearing Ann Arbor, I slowed down some. I had the name of my dorm, but I wasn't sure exactly where it was. Then I heard a sound from the back of the car. It was sort of like a muffled sneeze.

I pulled over to the side of the road and looked down at the back seat. Everything seemed normal, even the dusty blanket I always kept in case someone falls asleep or gets cold. Then, just on an impulse, I reached down and pulled the blanket off the floor of the car. There, huddled up in a ball, her head between her knees, was Taffy, "Oh, no," I said.

She didn't even move, like she thought maybe I wouldn't notice her if she kept quiet. "Taffy, what are you doing there?"

Still no answer. I reached down and shook her. "Hey! I mean it. Is this some kind of joke? I'm going to college. How're you going to get home?"

Slowly, she raised her head and stared at me, looking frightened. "I'm not going home," she said.

"Then, where're you going?"

"I want to be with you," Taffy said. "Please let me. I want it so much!"

"Taffy, come on. You know I'm starting college. And how about Linc and your baby? Do they know where you are?"

She shook her head.

"They're probably crazy with worry by now. You can't do this to them! Or to me."

"Oh, they don't care," Taffy said. "They don't care what happens to me."

"Sure they do," I said. "They love you."

"Not the way you do," Taffy said.

I took a deep breath. "I don't love you. I can't. I told you that."

"That night in the garden you said you did."

I leaned back, feeling miserable. "That was just . . . that was a mistake. You're Linc's wife, he's my friend. Don't you see—"

"You don't even have to love me," Taffy said. "All I want is to live near you and see you. You don't even have to speak to me. You can date other girls, whatever you want!"

"What would you live on? Where would you get the money?"

"I have some saved." Her face had a bright, gleaming intensity. "I'll get a job as a waitress or something. I don't *care* how I live. I can live just in some little room somewhere."

I realized I was in some kind of big trouble and that it would take a lot talking just to get Taffy to agree to go back home again. "Hey, let's get out and talk," I said. "Okay? It's stuffy in the car."

"Okay, sure." She popped up out of the back seat

and scrambled off to sit next to me by the side of the road. Cars were whizzing by.

"Have you had anything to eat since we left home?" I asked. She was sitting on the grass, her knees up, hugging herself.

Taffy shook her head. "I thought I'd wait till we arrived. I am a little hungry, but not too much."

"How'd you get in the car, anyway?"

"I was waiting in the bushes. While you went in to get your bags, I jumped in. I had it all planned out. It's all I've thought about for weeks." She looked pleased with herself. "How come you stopped at that other house just as you were setting off?"

"Just—I had to pick something up," I said.

"I thought I was going to suffocate till you finally opened the window," Taffy said, pulling on her pony tail. "Now I feel fine."

I hesitated. "Taff, how about . . . how about your baby? Don't you love him at least? I mean, you're his mother."

Taffy frowned. "I'm terrible!" she said. "I'm a terrible mohter! He's *always* screaming. It's like he hates life *already* and he's just six months old. And he's getting it from me. I'm a bad influence. Linc can marry someone else. He can marry Nancy or Sandra. Sandra always liked him."

"He doesn't *want* anyone else," I said. "He wants *you*. . . . And anyhow, all babies scream, but if you left, he'd miss you a whole lot. You're his mother."

Taffy shook her head in a hopeless, angry way. "What do *you* know about babies?" she said. "You don't know anything! You've never even had one."

"I know they need their own mother around," I said.

"They need someone," Taffy said, "but how do they know if it's their mother or their aunt or who. Anyhow, Spence, I've thought about that, too. This isn't just some hare-brained thing. I'll get my job and, if Linc doesn't want the baby, I'll send for him and he can live with me."

She was talking like the baby was a parcel that could arrive in the mail. "I don't think it's a good idea."

Taffy was staring ahead. "We'll work it out." She turned to look at me. "Remember how Ms. Emery used to say that the main key to happiness was first to figure out what made you happy and second to go about setting that up? Well, being with you is what makes me happy, and so I set it up."

"But it doesn't make *me* happy," I said, sighing. "Can't you understand that?"

"What do you mean?" She looked apprehensive.

"I can't have someone following me around all day. I'll be trying to go to classes. I have to study hard or I might lose my scholarship."

Taffy was poking at the ground with a stick. "I'm not just going to follow you around," she whispered. "How can you say that? I won't get in your way. You won't even know I'm there."

"But that's no life for you!" I said desperately. "Sneaking around, peeking at me from behind bushes. That won't make you happy. Besides, Taff, I told you this, I'm not like you think I am. I'm not that different from Linc."

"You are," Taffy insisted, jabbing the stick into the ground. "I know you. You're not like him at *all*."

"If we were married, I'd be just like Linc," I said. "I'd be distracted and irritable, I'd yell at you sometimes. You wouldn't be any happier than you are now."

Taffy beamed her big bluish eyes at me. "But we'd make love and it would be wonderful, like it was that night in the garden, and we'd both be so happy."

"No, we wouldn't! First of all, sometimes it'd be good and sometimes it'd be lousy. Sex is just one thing in life." My words sounded ironical, given what I'd been thinking about most of the time over the past month or so. "It's not all that important."

"It is if you love someone," Taffy said.

I looked out at the road. The light was fading, but it wasn't twilight. "Taff, I'm going to drive us to a rest place and call Linc and have him come and get you. Okay! I just can't take all this. It's been a hard summer for me in some ways, my grandfather dying, my grandmother acting crazy . . . I just plain can't take this!" My voice started shaking. I was afraid I might break down.

Taffy leapt to her feet. "No!" she cried. "I won't go back! You can't make me! I won't."

"You have to."

"If I can't be with you, I want to die," she said. "I'm going to die!" And, saying that, she ran right out in the middle of the highway. Just at that second a car was coming along on the other side of the road. He saw Taffy and swerved violently to one side, careening off into a ditch. Another car, coming from the other direction, seeing what had happened, slowed down and pulled to a halt. I ran out after Taffy who was dancing around the road, waving her arms, shouting, "I want to die! Run me over!" I pulled her off the road where the first car was stuck. The driver came out and looked at her with horror.

"What's going on?" he said. "We have a child in this car! She could have been hurt. What's going on?"

"Why didn't you run me over?" Taffy shouted at him? "I wanted you to kill me."

The man looked at me. "Who is this? Your sister? Your girlfriend?"

"She ran away from home," I said. My mouth was so dry I had trouble speaking. "I'm going to take her back."

At that point the driver of the other car, a tall thin man in a suit, came over. "I'll call an ambulance," he said.

"No one's hurt," the other man said. "It's a mental case."

"I've got a CB radio," the first man said. "Are you all right?" he asked Taffy. "Any concussion?"

The other man said, "She wasn't in the car! Listen to me, will you? She's crazy. She made me swerve off the road. My baby could've been killed."

"Why didn't you kill me?" Taffy said, weeping. "Why?"

The first man went back to his car to call someone on the CB radio. Then he came back with a flask of whiskey. "You have a little drink of this, honey," he said to Taffy. "You'll feel better in a minute."

To my surprise, Taffy took a long drink. "Why didn't you kill me?" she said to him, handing it back.

"Why would I do a thing like that?" he said. "To a lovely young girl. Think how your boyfriend here would feel."

"He's not my boyfriend," Taffy said, looking at me with red, wounded eyes. "He's just someone I used to love a long time ago."

The man kept talking to Taffy in a quiet, soothing voice. I went over and sat down next to my car.

Eventually a police car stopped near us. First, he helped the car out of the ditch, took everyone's license, listened to a babbled version of what had happened from everyone. Finally he turned to me. "Now, which is your car, young man?"

I pointed to it.

"And you say this woman was a passenger in your car?"

"Yes, sir, but I didn't realize it at the time. That's why I pulled over." I glanced at Taffy who was sitting on the side of the road, leaning against a tree, with her eyes closed. I couldn't tell if she was asleep or sick or what. I also wasn't sure if I'd committed some kind of crime, without even knowing it.

"You say you were in school together?"

"Yes, sir."

"She's your girlfriend?"

"No, sir. She's married to my best friend, one of my best friends. She has a six-month-old baby. She lives in Riverview."

"And why was she accompanying you on this trip?"

"She thinks she's in love with me. But she isn't really. And, well, she got upset."

"I wanted to be run over," Taffy said quietly. She opened her eyes and looked at the police officer. "Would you run me over?"

"No, I don't think I'd want to do that," he said. To me he said, "Why don't the two of you come into town with us and we'll try and straighten things out."

"How about my car?" I said. "I don't want to just leave it on the highway."

"My partner'll bring it in for you." He went over to Taffy. "Okay, young lady, we're going to take a nice little drive into town now, me, your boyfriend and you."

"He's not my boyfriend!" Taffy said. But, to my surprise, she followed the officer obediently, like a dog, not even looking at me.

In the car Taffy sat silently between me and the police officer, her hands folded in her lap. "Starting school?" he asked me.

"Right," I said. I didn't feel much like talking.

"It's a fine school, the best." He glanced at Taffy. "Don't worry. Everything'll be okay."

Back at the station house the officer asked me if I wanted to call Taffy's family. I knew I had to, so I did. Linc was at home. I explained what had happened to him, but not in too much detail because Taffy was sitting nearby. "I think she's—"

"Yeah," he said. "I know."

By then it was seven in the evening. I felt so exhausted I was ready to drop. I asked the officer if I could try and find my dorm and get some supper. I promised to come back afterward. Taffy had fallen asleep. They brought her inside and laid her down on a flat cot in someone's office. She was lying curled on her side, her hand in front of her mouth, breathing peacefully.

# 20

I still have bad dreams about Taffy, even now, four months after it happened. She'll start screaming, "Run me over! Run me over!" and I'll be in this big car that's somehow out of control, no brakes. Sometimes the car catches fire, sometimes, to avoid hitting her, I have to swerve to one side. I always wake up in a cold sweat.

Linc and his family decided to put Taffy in some kind of mental hospital, but then her parents took her out and brought her home. They had to promise the doctor they'd took after her and not let her do any harm to herself. Linc wrote me that he wanted to go see her, but her parents didn't think it would be such a good idea. Some afternoons, he says, her mother gets the baby and Taffy plays with him and seems to like him, but when they take him away, she doesn't seem to care much. She doesn't think it's her baby. She always says to thank the mother for letting her play with him.

I think she's more or less forgotten about me. At least she never talks about me anymore. Linc says I was just what triggered it off, that she was an unstable person and it wasn't my fault. "Our marriage was over anyway," he said. "I don't know if we ever even *had* a marriage." He sounds pretty embittered and angry when he talks about it. His mother and Taffy's mother have both said they'll raise the baby and he can go off to school if he wants, but he says right now he doesn't have the heart for it. "So, how're you liking it?" he asked.

I was home for the weekend, even though it wasn't Thanksgiving yet. I was just staying for the weekend. "The work's real hard," I said. "I'm not doing that well."

I could tell that pleased him, though he tried not to show it. "Well, it'll probably pick up next semester," he said.

What I see now is how easy it is, comparatively, to be one of the best at a small-town high school like ours. Michigan is hard enough to get into that practically all the kids are bright and a lot of them work hard, especially those who're pre-med. I started out thinking I could work the way I did in high school, doing papers at the last minute, putting off studying things I couldn't understand. But that doesn't work. It all backslides till you have so much to do, you don't know where to start. Also, though I don't want to make excuses for myself, I haven't been in the greatest frame of mind mentally.

"Want to go out for a beer tonight?" Linc asked.

"Just a quick one," I said. "I should get home to my grandmother."

I met him at Veronica's. As I walked in, I saw Linc

with a girl. At first I thought it was Taffy, because she had the same color hair and roughly the same build. But as I came closer, I saw it wasn't. "This is Jill," Linc said. "Jill, my old buddy, Spencer."

I sat down opposite both of them and took a quick glance at Jill. She wasn't as pretty as Taffy, but she had nice shiny long hair. "I hear you're at Michigan," she said. "My sister's there. She's a freshman, too. Did you ever run into her? Marjorie Vance?"

I shook my head. "The classes are pretty big."

"She says the work is real hard. Well, I'm not even going to try out for it. My grades aren't good enough."

Linc said, "Jill's at Riverview. She's a junior."

"I used to see you guys," she said. "But you seemed so much older, so full of yourselves . . ." She laughed.

"Then one day we ran into each other here," Linc said. "Jill's terrific at bowling. You wouldn't even think she was a girl, if you saw her swing."

Jill flexed her arm. "I'm muscle-bound," she said, though in fact she just looked in good shape. "My mom says it'll keep boys away."

"Not a chance," Linc said.

He kept looking at me for approval, like he wanted me to like her, and think he was quite a guy for finding her. And it wasn't that I didn't like her. If I'd met her in any other circumstance, I'd have felt fine. But the thought of Taffy made the whole situation painful for me. I kept thinking of her that day on the road, full of all those crazy plans that she must've known, on some level, were crazy, or the way she'd looked curled up in the police station, her hand in front of her mouth.

When we went to the men's room later, Linc said, "How'd you like her? Isn't she great?"

"Yeah, she's nice," I said. I gave him a cold stare. "Aren't you still married, though?"

"What? The thing with Taffy? She's not a wife, she's just a nut case. Okay, I didn't mean it that way, but she can hardly, well, satisfy many of my needs, if you get what I'm saying. And personally I don't think we'll get back together, even if she does improve. What's in it for me?"

"Nothing, if you don't love her, I guess," I said.

I saw some guy watching us, overhearing our conversation.

"It's all over," Linc said. "And Jill is great about it. She says she had an aunt like that, that was always flipping in and out. Maybe it's genetic or something."

I wasn't feeling well. I'd drunk two or three beers too fast and I felt cold and clammy, as though the walls of the men's room were moving slowly closer, then further away, like I was in the middle of an accordion. "I have to go," I said.

When I got outside, it was chilly. I leaned against the car and heaved up in the bushes. After that, though I hate throwing up, I felt better. Weak and with that awful sour taste in my mouth, but better.

When I got back home, my grandmother was getting ready to go to sleep. She was in her flannel nightgown. She says she's sleeping better now and sometimes even makes it through the night. The photo's still there, but she doesn't talk to it anymore, not that I've noticed anyway.

"Did you have a nice evening, dear?" she asked, just as though I were back in high school.

"Yeah, I just . . . I met some friends." My

grandmother knows about Taffy and has even gone to visit her, but we haven't talked about it and I don't especially want to.

I lay in bed a long, long time, unable to fall asleep. I thought not only of Taffy, but of the letter I got from Audrey the first week I was at school. I tore it up and threw it out, but I can still remember every word. She wrote:

Dear Spence,

I know I didn't handle our last meeting together the way I should've. I'm a coward, I guess. There was something I wanted to tell you that explains why I acted funny the last few times we were together. It's that Mike and I are going to try getting back together again. When I met him I was just a kid, only sixteen. I really was too young to know what I was doing and I gave him a hard time. But now I think I'm ready to try again. Not that I'm going to settle down and be Harriet Housewife. I still have my dreams about being a pilot. Maybe that's all they'll be— dreams—but I'm not giving up yet. I have a job in a travel agency here in Oakland, and Mike's working too so we're doing okay. There's a flying school not far from here and I drive down sometimes and look at the planes, talk to some of the pilots. Maybe one day, way in the future you'll be flying somewhere and you'll hear my voice over the loudspeaker!

Spence, I know you're going to think I was just using you, just having fun for the summer, but it wasn't just that. I know there's no way I can prove that to you, but it's the truth. You're such a sweet person, but you remind me of myself five years ago. I know you've got some growing up to do and you need lots of time to think things through. Maybe by the time you get this, you'll have found a new girlfriend. I hope so. I envy her. I'll always remember you. Thanks, sweetie, for all you gave me.

Much love,
Audrey

I've had quite a few bad moments in the past few months, but none where I felt quite as rotten as I did after reading that letter. The closeness I had with Audrey—true, it had quite a lot of what my grandmother would call a "physical aspect" to it—but it was a hell of a lot more than just that. We talked about things I've never talked about with other girls, or even with guys. Maybe because she was a little older or had seen more of the world than I had, I felt like she could give me advice about things. Most of the time she did it in a concerned, friendly way, not condescending. That's why this letter really hurt.

I think I'm going to stay away from girls for a while, certainly in any serious way. Especially if I want to get good grades and get into a good med school. One day on campus I ran into Janice, that girl who tempted me with a beer the day I was fixing the light fixture for Mercer. She stopped me and flirted and asked me about my courses. Maybe, if my mood had been different, I'd have said, Sure, why not give it a try. But I just made up a bunch of excuses and I haven't called her, even though she gave me her phone number.

I don't want to sound conceited but, if I'd had any

desire to, I could've made it with plenty of girls by now. Some of them come on pretty strong. Maybe it's being away from home, where they don't have to worry about what their parents think. One day some girl whose name I didn't even *know* followed me out of the shower with just a towel wrapped around her and asked if I had a French-English dictionary she could borrow! I've heard of lame excuses before, but that about takes the cake.

There's one girl in my dorm who's more of a friend than anything else—Alyssa Wall. She's pre-med too, and she got crummy grades the first quarter also. The day she got them, she knocked on my door and said, crossing her eyes, "Spence, convince me not to jump off a cliff." When I showed her my grades, she said she felt a lot better. It was the same for her as it was for me; she comes from a small town and was the editor of the school paper, all As, captain of the girls' basketball team. "Here I am a nothing squared," she said. "I look in the mirror twice a day just to make sure I exist."

"I know exactly how you feel," I said.

I don't think I'll have any trouble of the kind I had with Audrey and Taffy with Alyssa: she's completely not my type, but she's a good friend, someone to talk to, like a guy but different, maybe a little like some of my sisters. I'm glad I met her, but it's not what you'd call a romantic situation.

When I came down for breakfast, I noticed my grandmother had my high school graduation photo, propped up in the window, facing out to the street. "Hey, what's that doing there?" I asked.

"Oh," she said in her wry, offhand way. "I thought you might like a view."

I stared at her. "But I'm alive! I'm right here! If I want a view, I can just look out the window."

She sighed. "I should have taken it down for your visit, I suppose," she said. "I knew you'd take on about it. It's just such a lovely photo. And I found it in the album and thought why keep it there, all stuffed away?"

"Why not put it on the piano?" I said.

"I like having it in the window," she said. "That way, when I come home, I look up and there you are, seeming to smile at me and ask, 'Did you have a nice day, Gran?' the way you used to in the old days."

I looked at my watch, for no good reason, since I had no special plans and wasn't intending to head back to college till noon.

My grandmother pointed her finger at me accusingly. "You think I'm living in the past. Don't bother to protest. I know that. Well, I'm not! What's past is past. Omar is gone, you're gone—not in the same way, I realize, but you're both not here and no one in the world is more aware of that than I am. I'm not some addle-brained old coot dressing up in my wedding dress to see if it still fits. But I don't see any harm in establishing some connection to the past. That's all it is—a connection."

"Sure," I said.

"Spencer, I am the most down-to-earth human being that ever trod the earth. It's a problem for me. I can't read poetry, I don't understand philosophy. Omar would try to go on about grand schemes of thought and I'll tell you truly, all I was thinking was, 'When will he let me go start fixing dinner.' So don't worry about me not knowing what's real and what isn't."

"I'm not Gran," I said quickly. "Maybe it's that I

never liked that photo of me. It doesn't look like me, exactly."

My grandmother took it down to gaze at it. "Well, it doesn't do you justice, that's true, but I can't tell you how many people have commented, perfect strangers. '*Who* is that handsome young man in your window?' Perhaps some thought I had a young beau." She laughed delightedly at the idea.

I went in and fixed myself a big breakfast while my grandmother chattered on in the background about how I shouldn't feel bad about my grades; she knew I would make it. "You have strength of character and good genes. That's what it takes, Spencer. And kindness. That helps, too."

Frankly, I don't know if any of these will get me into med school, but I kept my mouth shut.

"I'll tell you what," my grandmother said when I was done. "Let's just drop over and look in on poor little Taffy before you go. What do you say? Just say hello."

"I don't think it would be such a good idea," I said. I was afraid Taffy might get upset seeing me.

"Just hello . . . she's perfectly calm now, dear, nothing like what she was. The doctor told her mother she just needs time to live quietly, no responsibilities, and after a while it'll all come back to her. Sometimes that happens, you know. You go along, living perfectly as you used to, and *boing*, the string breaks. That happens to most of us at some point."

"Well, I can only stay a minute," I said.

"Only a minute," my grandmother echoed.

Maybe it was because of Taffy visiting her right after my grandfather's death that my grandmother had taken to going to see her. We drove up to Taffy's parents' house. It's small, not that fancy, with just a little garden off to the side. Taffy was sitting on the front porch, with some kind of knitting in her lap. When she saw me, she got a frightened expression; then she looked calm again.

"Spencer is due back at college any minute now, but he's come to say hello," my grandmother said, pulling up a chair.

"Hi," I said, trying to look normal.

Taffy just looked at me. "You're in college?" she said.

"Yeah, well, it's hard, harder than I thought. My grades weren't so good the first semester."

"But they'll probably get better," Taffy said tonelessly. She was talking like I was someone she'd never seen before. Then she looked at my grandmother. "I'm feeling a lot better today, Mrs. Searles."

"Oh, I'm so glad, dear," my grandmother said warmly. "Good for you."

Taffy's eyes clung to me. "I've been ill," she said. "That's why I'm here at my parents' house. But pretty soon *I'm* going to start applying to college."

"Where are you thinking of?" my grandmother asked.

"I don't know yet," Taffy said. "I want to be a pilot, eventually, so I have to go someplace that's good for that."

"A pilot?" my grandmother said. "Well, how brave of you! How adventurous! I'm scared even to fly from here to Detroit." Then she turned to me. "Didn't you have a friend who wanted to be a pilot, Spencer? I can't recall exactly."

I turned red. "I—I don't know," I stammered.

"That was me," Taffy said, leaning forward. Her nails were all bitten way far down. "I was his friend."

My grandmother's face looked troubled. "Well, and you still are, aren't you?" She turned to me for confirmation.

"Sure," I said. "You're still my friend, Taffy."

Then Taffy just sat there, staring at me. It was a long, sorrowful, detached stare, almost as though I were someone she'd known from years ago and was trying to remember. Suddenly I couldn't take it. I jumped to my feet. "I really have to go," I said.

Taffy got up, too. "You have a long trip ahead of you," she said, in that same funny flat voice. She reached out and shook my hand. "It was kind of you to drop by."

"Well, take care," I said awkwardly. Her hand was cold.

I'd already packed the car. I drove my grandmother back to the house, but neither of us spoke till we got there. "Be good!" she called as I drove off. "Drive carefully! Write!"

Behind my grandmother I saw the photo of myself, smiling confidently out at the empty street, looking as though there was no problem in the world I couldn't solve. Then I turned the corner and headed onto the thruway, back to college.

## About the Author

Norma Klein is the immensely popular author of novels for adults, young adults and children. Her books for Fawcett include ANGEL FACE, BEGINNERS' LOVE, IT'S OKAY IF YOU DON'T LOVE ME, LOVE IS ONE OF THE CHOICES, THE QUEEN OF WHAT IFS, BIZOU and SNAPSHOTS.

Ms. Klein grew up in New York City. She lives on the Upper West Side of Manhattan with her husband and two teenage daughters.